ISBN 978-1-331-28185-6
PIBN 10168606

This book is a reproduction of an important historical work. Forgotten Books uses
state-of-the-art technology to digitally reconstruct the work, preserving the original format
whilst repairing imperfections present in the aged copy. In rare cases, an imperfection in
the original, such as a blemish or missing page, may be replicated in our edition. We do,
however, repair the vast majority of imperfections successfully; any imperfections that
remain are intentionally left to preserve the state of such historical works.

English
Français
Deutsche
Italiano
Español
Português

www.forgottenbooks.com

Mythology Photography **Fiction**
Fishing Christianity **Art** Cooking
Essays Buddhism Freemasonry
Medicine **Biology** Music **Ancient
Egypt** Evolution Carpentry Physics
Dance Geology **Mathematics** Fitness
Shakespeare **Folklore** Yoga Marketing
Confidence Immortality Biographies
Poetry **Psychology** Witchcraft
Electronics Chemistry History **Law**
Accounting **Philosophy** Anthropology
Alchemy Drama Quantum Mechanics
Atheism Sexual Health **Ancient History**
Entrepreneurship Languages Sport
Paleontology Needlework Islam
Metaphysics Investment Archaeology
Parenting Statistics Criminology
Motivational

THE

IS BECK

THE JALASCO
BRIG

BY

LOUIS BECKE

AUTHOR OF "TOM WALLIS"; "BY REEF AND PALM"; "RODMAN
THE BOATSTEERER"; "THE STRANGE ADVENTURE OF JAMES
SHERVINTON"; "BREACHLEY, BLACK SHEEP";
"BY ROCK AND POOL"; ETC.

LONDON
ANTHONY TREHERNE & CO., LTD.
3 AGAR STREET, STRAND, W.C.
1902

CONTENTS

LIST OF ILLUSTRATIONS

THE JALASCO
BRIG

———◆———

CHAPTER I.

NEARLY a thousand miles north and west of
Samoa, in the South Pacific, is a cluster of
seven and thirty lovely palm-clad islands
enclosing a spacious lagoon, marked on the
charts as De Peyster's Island, but called by
the people who dwell there Nukufetau,
which signifies "the land of the *fetau* [1]
tree," for of all the scores of groups and
isolated clusters of low-lying coral islands
in the North and South Pacific, Nukufetau
exceeds them all in the size and beauty of
the *fetau* trees, which there thrive well on

[1] *Callophyllum Inophyllum.*

the rich and soft but shallow soil, formed
by the falling leaves of many hundreds of
years mixing with decayed coral detritus,
and continuously moistened by the warm
tropical rain.

In the days of which I write—not much
more than sixty years ago—a full thousand
of vigorous, healthy and warlike brown
people lived on the thirty-seven islands,
and, all day long, canoes with great lateen
sails of mats sailed to and fro across the
lagoon from one island to another, carrying
visitors from village to village, the men
armed with heavy iron-wood clubs, and
swords, and daggers set with sharks' teeth,
or long, slender spears made from the coco-
nut tree; the women and girls nude · to
the waist, with wreaths of sweet smelling
flowers encircling their heads, or suspended
from their necks; and at night time, when
the houses were in darkness, long lines of
fires could be seen on every beach as the
people of each village brought out their

mats and spread them on the sand to sit
and watch the young men and women dance
their wild dances of the fierce old heathen
days, and hear the tales of those who, ten
years before, had sailed with the great
Foilapé in his fleet of fifty canoes to the
island of Nui, where he slew six hundred
people, men, women, and children, and
brought their skulls home to Nukufetau to
adorn the temple of the god Erikobai. But
now Foilapé was dead, and his name might
be spoken by even the lips of a child;
though in his life, when he ruled the land
with a bloody hand, even his bravest and
most trusted warriors dared not speak to
him but in a whisper, and with head bent
low. And so now because that the terror
of Foilapé was gone from their hearts, and
a new chief who was less cruel and avari-
cious reigned in his stead, the people of the
thirty-seven isles made merry, though ever
prepared for war with those of their race on
Nui to the north, and Funafuti, to the south.

But all this is changed now, and the rattle of the wooden war drum has given place to the sound of the mission school bell, calling them together in the big white-walled church built of coral lime and stones, taken from the reef; and the remaining people of the group, especially those of the younger generation, know nothing of the heathen laws, customs, and mode of life of their savage forefathers. All they do know is that those were the times of the *po uli uli*—the old heathen days, when men's lives were held cheaply, and when the whispered word or the open frown of the chief, and the ill-will of the priests of the god Erikobai, meant swift death by club or spear.

.   .   .   .   .

One morning soon after daylight, about eleven years after the despot Foilapé had fled for his life to the neighbouring island of Vaitupu, a weather-worn brig made her appearance off the entrance leading into the lagoon, and, to the astonishment of the natives, without waiting for a pilot, sailed confidently in through the dangerous passage, and dropped her anchor off the principal village, which was situated on the fertile island of Teanamu. In a few minutes she was surrounded by a number of canoes, each trying to get alongside first, when the captain, who was standing on the poop, called out to them in English not to be in such a hurry. There was plenty of time, he said, as the ship wanted wood and water, and would remain in the lagoon for at least ten days. Could any of them speak English? he asked.

"Yes," replied a fine, stalwart young native named Fonu ('The Turtle'), "I can speak English, and there are some more men here who can speak it, but not speak it good like me."

"Well, you and those with you come aboard, and tell the others that they can have a look at the ship some other time.

I don't want my decks filled with people to-day. My crew are tired, and need rest, for we have had bad weather, and the ship is leaking so much that I may have to put her on the beach here."

This was good news for the natives, who knew that in all probability their services would be required in beaching the brig, and that they would be paid for their assistance in firearms and ammunition, tobacco, and fiery rum—the staple articles of trade in the South Seas in those wild days. That the brig was no ordinary trading ship they could see, for she carried ten guns, though manned by a very small crew. With such ships it was the custom —similar to that observed in the Society and Marquesas Islands—for every man of the crew to choose some particular native for his *soa*[1] or friend, and when the time came for the ship's departure, a mutual

[1] Synonymous with the Tahitian *Taio* and the Samoan *uo*.

interchange of presents took place. The ·seamen would give their *soas* such useful and greatly desired articles as sheath-knives, nails, metal buttons, etc., and would receive in return, mats, native head-dresses, turtle shells, and other curios.

The moment Fonu stepped on board he shook hands with the captain, and then looked around him in admiration; for the brig, although heavily armed, and despite the small crew she carried, was in such excellent order, that her decks and guns equalled in their smart appearance those of any man-of-war he had ever seen.

"Is this ship man-o'-war?" he asked.

"No," replied the master of the brig, with a laugh, "but she was built to be a man-of-war, and was fitted out as one—that is why she has so many guns. When I bought her I bought the guns as well. Now, come below, my friend, and have a glass of grog, and I'll tell you what I want done."

The native followed him into the main cabin, which was handsomely fitted up, and bidding him be seated, the captain called for liquor, and poured out some brandy into his visitor's glass. Then in a few minutes he told him what he required.

"I shall want wood and water, as I said. But first I need a lot of men—fifty at least —to help my crew to take the guns from the decks and all heavy things from the hold on shore, so that she can be put upon the beach. We struck on a reef many weeks ago, and I think she's pretty badly hurt. Can you get the men for me?"

"The chief will do all you want," replied Fonu, who, however, went on to say that before the chief could undertake such an operation he would have to consult Potiri, the head priest, who was practically the ruler of the whole lagoon. The priest, he explained, would, after the captain had made his requirements known, consult the oracle in the temple, and if the shades of certain deified ancestors of the people gave a favourable answer, the work would be at once proceeded with. But, the young native ingenuously added, it all depended upon what presents the captain made to Potiri, independent of what he paid the people for their labour.

"Ah, I see," said the captain, stroking his beard thoughtfully. "What do you think this chap Potiri would like?"

"Guns, powder and ball, red cloth, knives, axes—all such things."

"Well, he shall have four new muskets with bayonets, a keg of bullets, a keg of powder, and a lot of knives. I have no red cloth, but can give him two red shirts. Will you tell him this for me?"

Fonu's dark eyes sparkled at the mere mention of such a gift, and said he would at once go on shore and speak to Potiri privately, before the captain paid his visit to the king. Then he inquired how it was that the brig was so easily able to enter the lagoon.

"One of my officers, who was here a long time ago in a whaleship, told me he could pilot me in, and that the people here would not try to capture my ship and kill us. But there was a ship cut off here once, wasn't there?"

Fonu replied frankly that the captain was correct. The ship was cut off and everyone on board killed. But that was long ago, when he was quite a little boy. Since then, no further attempt had ever been made, for the people now desired only to trade, and not fight with and kill white men. There were, he said, three or four men on Nuku-fetau who could speak English. They had been to sea in whaleships; he himself, he added proudly, had been eleven years in English and American whaling and trading ships, and had been to Sydney, London and New Bedford.

As an indication of his goodwill, the

The Captain made him a present of some tobacco and a naval uniform."

[*See page* 17.

captain then made the native a present of some tobacco and a naval uniform much ornamented with tarnished gold lace. Then, promising to meet the captain on shore and conduct him to the chief, the young man took his departure.

As soon as he had left the cabin, the captain called the Chileno steward.

"Tell Mr. Merrill I want him."

A few minutes later, Merrill, the mate of the brig, entered the cabin, and carefully closing the door, seated himself opposite the captain.

CHAPTER II.

No two men more unlike in personal appearance and manners could be imagined than Captain Benjamin Rowley and his chief mate, Thomas Merrill. The former was tall, stout, broad shouldered and bearded, talked volubly and was careless, almost dirty in his dress; Merrill was short, slender, clean-shaven, particularly neat in his clothing, which fitted him perfectly, whereas Rowley's garments looked as if they had been cut out with a knife and fork and fitted by a one-armed tailor.

"Well, Ben," said Merrill with an unmistakable American accent, "how did you get on?"

"First rate, first rate, Tom," replied the captain, leaning back in his chair, and squaring his huge shoulders; "take a drink, and I'll tell you all about it."

The American helped himself sparingly to some brandy, and then lighting a cigar, listened carefully to Rowley's account of his interview with Fonu.

"So you see, Tom, we'll get along all right with these people here, and what Kingston said he had heard of them is true, so he has played fair with us. What is he doing now?"

"Nothing particular. I was waiting to see what you wanted done."

The captain considered for a few moments, and then turned his ruddy, rather pleasant looking face to his officer, and said as he laid his hand upon the table—

"Look here, Tom Merrill. You and me have been together a long time now, and you know the kind of customer I am, and that I've done some queer things in my time—tougher jobs than collaring this brig, as you know—and my conscience is pretty elastic; but I *don't* like—no, I'm hanged if I like—the idea of treating him badly. It 'goes agin me,' as you Yankees say."

Merrill nodded. "Well, what are you going to do? I reckon *I* don't bear the man any ill-will. He's as good a sailor man as ever chewed dead horse meat and wanted to buy a farm."

"We *must* make him come in with us, Tom. I'll try him again."

"Guess you might as well try to teach a buffalo how to make buckwheat cakes. He won't do it. If it wasn't for the girl he'd have more sense."

"Ah, that's it. I didn't act square with him, in the first place, when I met him that night in Arica; and then, as you say, the girl is always in his mind. But I'll try him again, Tom. I can't bring myself to put him ashore on any of these islands, and yet what are we to do? We must have someone to navigate."

Something like a smile flickered across the American's face. "We're a mighty poor pair of pirates, Ben. What you ought to have done in the first place was to have sounded him carefully, and when you found he was not the sort of man we wanted looked for someone else. But you didn't, and so there's no use talking about it. And unless we put him ashore somewhere between here and the Bonin Islands—at some island where ships are few and far between—we'll make a mess of things. And what is more, if he gets a ghost of a chance to recapture the ship he will try to do it."

"He will, Tom," said Rowley, gloomily; "but I think the men know you and me too well to let him try it on."

Merrill's hard, saturnine yet handsome features relaxed, and a grim smile moved his lips. "They do, and they well know, too, that none of them can put foot ashore again anywhere between Valdivia and Callao. No, Ben, the men are all right. Kingston, I am pretty sure, has tried to sound them, once since the nigger disappeared and once since we lost the steward, although they have said nothing about it to us."

Rowley made no remark. He was thinking deeply. Then after helping himself, he pushed the decanter of brandy towards Merrill. They drank together in silence. Then the mate rose to go on deck.

"Set the hands to unbend sails, Tom," said the captain; "the sooner we get her on the beach the better. I'll fix up matters with the natives, and be back before dinnertime. Now tell Kingston I want to see him. I'll try him once more."

Captain Rowley sat waiting impatiently, drumming the cabin table with his fingers. Then, as the man he was expecting entered the cabin, he motioned him to a seat.

The newcomer was a man of about thirty

years of age, dressed in the usual style of
merchant officers of those days. His face,
neck, and hands were tanned a deep
reddish-bronze by long years of exposure
under torrid suns and wild skies, and his
features, though handsome, were somewhat
too lined and stern for a man of his years;
and as his grey, deep-set eyes met those
of Rowley, the latter, who had plenty of
assurance and bull-dog pluck, felt something like a blush creep up to his temples.

"Won't you take a glass of grog, Mr.
Kingston?" he began, somewhat shame-
facedly.

"No, I won't. I'm going to lend the
mate a hand. He tells me you wish to
unbend sails."

"Yes, I do. And then I'll put the brig
on the beach; but first I want to talk to
you, Mr. Kingston."

"Well, go ahead, but don't spin it out too
long," said Kingston, looking him squarely
in the face again.

"Look here, Kingston," said Rowley, rising from his seat, and placing both hands on the table, "I ask you for the last time. Won't you join us? A third share of the plunder, man."

"And I tell you for the last time that I'll see you and your fellow pirate hanged—and by heavens you deserve to be hanged—before I will have anything to do with you and Merrill and your Chileno gaol birds, and share any of your plunder."

Captain Rowley's face purpled. "Stop," he said hoarsely; "for your own sake don't try me too far. Look here, man—I mean well to you; by heaven I do. You saved my life in the Paumotus, and——"

"And you have ruined mine," retorted Kingston fiercely. "I was a fool to do it. I should have let you drown."

"Don't drive me to desperation," breathed rather than spoke Rowley. "I am a desperate —and a dangerous man. For your own sake——"

"Do what you please," and with a defiant glance, Kingston strode from the cabin and went on deck.

Shortly afterwards Rowley appeared, followed by one of the Chileno seamen, who was carrying a number of articles intended as a preliminary present for the chief. One of the quarter-boats was lowered and manned by half a dozen men, and Captain Rowley taking his seat, set off for the shore.

At the landing place the boat was met by Fonu and some of the leading men of the island, by whom the captain was conducted to the *fale kaupule*, or council house, where the head chief and his *kaupule* or councillors awaited him. After the usual florid compliments—which all Malayo-Polynesians are fond of paying and receiving—had been exchanged through Fonu, who acted as interpreter, Rowley made his request for assistance to enable him to repair his ship, and named the number of muskets, etc., which he would

give in return. As Fonu had told him, the
chief replied that he and his people were
quite willing to do all that was desired, but
that the head priest, Potiri, would first have
to consult the oracle of the gods; the
captain, however, should have an answer
by sunrise on the following day.

This finished the interview, and Rowley,
whose herculean proportions were greatly
admired by the people, returned to the ship,
accompanied by Fonu, quite satisfied, for
the young native informed him that he had
seen Potiri, who would not fail to tell the
people that the gods wished them to render
every assistance and hospitality to the
white men.

So, as soon as he reached the deck, he
instructed Merrill to send down the royal
masts, topmasts, upper yards, and have
all ready to haul the brig on to the shore
early on the following morning.

At supper time, much to his and Merrill's
surprise, Kingston seemed to have quite

forgotten the morning's brief altercation between the captain and himself, and conversed freely with them both, displaying an interest in Rowley's account of his reception by the natives, and of Potiri's priestly power. Then he inquired if he (Rowley) had been told by the natives which was the best spot to beach the vessel.

"They want me to haul her in right abreast of the village," replied the burly captain, " but I don't like the place at all; it would suit them of course, and that's all they care about, but there's not enough 'fall' from the water's edge, and I'm afraid we can't get at her keel if we put her there."

" What about that flat stretch of reef in front of those two little islands," suggested Kingston, with unusual affability; " it was quite dry there when we anchored this morning; and at high water there must be a good eight or ten feet of water on it."

"Just the very place!" exclaimed

Rowley. "I'll go and look at it in the morning."

Just before sundown, the captain again went on shore, and returned rather late in the evening. Kingston was walking the deck, smoking his pipe.

"That was a good idea of yours, Mr. Kingston," said Rowley; "even the natives, though they wanted me badly to put the ship on the beach right in front of the village, say that the place you saw is the best; it is hard, smooth rock, and we can work better at her there than on soft, sandy mud."

Then he paused, and said with a certain affected bluntness—"I think I'll have a tot and turn in. Won't you join. me?"

"Thank you, I will," replied Kingston, affably. And secretly delighted at the second officer's change of demeanour, Rowley led the way into the cabin, where the two remained for quite half an hour,

talking on various matters, but each carefully avoiding any allusion to the cause of
disagreement between them.

Then bidding each other good-night,
Rowley went to his state room, and
Kingston, whose mind was full of a project
which had come to him but a few hours
before, went on deck to think it out un-
disturbedly.

And as Kingston paced to and fro on
the quarter-deck, Rowley tapped at the
mate's open door, and Merrill sat up in his
bunk.

"I think he's coming round, Tom," said
the captain in a whisper.

"Maybe," said Merrill, pessimistically;
"reckon we can't tell till we know for
certain. Good-night."

CHAPTER III.

THE night was wondrously bright and calm, and Kingston, as he paced to and fro on the quarter-deck, busied as he was with his own thoughts, could not but gaze upon the beauties of the scene before him. The brig lay motionless upon the sleeping lagoon, which save for the occasional ripple or splash caused by a fish sleeting to the surface was as smooth as a sheet of glass and reflected upon its bosom the steady light of myriad stars.

Astern, and within half a mile, the clustered houses of the native village stood out sharp and clear with a background of tall palms lifting their pluméd heads against

the western sky. In front of the village, on
a beach of snow-white sand, lay a long row
of canoes, on which women and children sat
and talked and sung, as they waited for the
men to come forth from the houses, and
launch their frail craft for the night's fishing
out beyond the wavering line of tumbling
surf which forever beat upon the barrier reef
a mile away. And then, on either hand of
the brig, as he turned his face for'ard, were
the curving, palm-fringed beaches of the
other isles encompassing the lagoon; with
here and there a faint glimmer of firelight
showing through the groves of some little
village nestled therein.

.   .   .   .   .

Less than two years before that evening,
Kingston had thought himself one of the
luckiest men in existence; for after sixteen
years of seafaring life in all quarters of the
globe, beginning as an ordinary seaman,
and working up to chief mate, he found
himself master of a fine brigantine em-

ployed in the West Coast of South America trade.

The brigantine was the *Rosa Forestier*, named after one of the daughters of the owner, a Captain Forestier of Valparaiso, one of the wealthiest merchants of that city. Kingston had joined the vessel by the merest chance.

Mate of a leaky coal-laden ship which had arrived at Valparaiso from an Australian port and had been condemned after survey, he found himself unable to get another ship unless he liked to sink his dignity and ship before the mast.

One day, after three weeks' idleness, he went to his lodgings, which were over a combined grocer's, ironmonger's, bookseller's and stationer's shop in the Almendral. The proprietor was an Englishman who had been long settled in the country. He would often, as Kingston passed through the shop, ask him to sit down and smoke a cigar. On this occasion, however, the

young seaman saw that there were cus-
tomers being attended to by his landlord—
a gentleman and three young ladies, who
were, he could see at a glance, English
people, and, indeed, as he passed by
them, raising his hat, he heard them
speaking in English. A few minutes after
he had entered his room, he was surprised
by his landlord coming to his door with
a smiling face.

"You've just come in at the right time.
Mr. Kingston. That is Captain Forestier.
He owns several vessels sailing out of here
and Concepcion. I happened to mention
that you wanted a ship, and he says he
should like to see you. So come along."

Kingston needed no pressing. He at
once followed the landlord, and was introduced to Forestier, a tall, keen-eyed
business-like man of sixty, and in five
minutes he was practically engaged as
master of the *Rosa Forestier*, whose captain
had died suddenly the day previously, just

as the vessel was on the point of sailing for Concepcion.

"When can you go aboard?" queried Forestier, in his sharp, abrupt manner, as he looked at Kingston under his bushy brows.

"At once."

"Ah, that's right. I'll go with you, and we'll call at the Custom House on our way. Speak Spanish?"

"Pretty well."

"Good. Now, sir, we'll go. Ah, I forgot. Mr. Kingston, my daughters. Your new command is named after my second daughter, Miss Rosa Forestier. Now, girls, drive home; don't wait for me."

Kingston had but one brief glance at Rosa Forestier's face. She was very lovely, he thought, lovelier than her two sisters, and he wondered whether he should see her again. Most probably not, he reflected. Her father did not look the sort of man

who would be likely to invite one of
his captains to visit his house, and anyway
what business had he, a man without a
dollar, to let any woman come into his
thoughts ?

With Forestier he boarded the brigantine, and was well satisfied with his first
command. On the following day he sailed
for Valdivia, with which place his employer
did a large trade, always sending there
every few months one of the six vessels
he owned.

From the very first Kingston met with
good luck and returned to Valparaiso much
sooner than Captain Forestier expected, and
was duly complimented upon the quick passage he had made. His next voyage was to
Callao, where Forestier had a branch of his
business, and on this occasion the merchant
himself came with him as supercargo.

During the voyage there and back, he
watched Kingston closely, and himself a
seaman of great experience, and used to the

controlling of rough and mutinous crews, he could not but admit to himself that in Edward Kingston he had found a man who though so young was every whit as capable and resourceful as was he himself in times of emergency and danger. When they returned to Valparaiso after a highly successful and profitable voyage, he invited Kingston to his house, introduced him to his friends, and eventually, as time went on, and the young captain's continuously successful trips raised him higher in his opinion, he desired him to consider his country house his home whenever the *Rosa Forestier* was in port.

For Captain Forestier never for one moment dreamt that Kingston, privileged guest as he was, would presume to lift his eyes to one of his daughters; had he entertained the slightest suspicion of such a thing, he would most certainly have brought that daring young man up with a round turn, and curtly told him that his services were no longer required. Always busied in his money-making, he never noticed that Rosa and Kingston were very often together, her mother and sisters, who all liked the handsome young sailor, giving them every opportunity of meeting. Before he had been a year in Forestier's employ, Kingston had one day spoken to Rosa of his love, and she had promised to be his wife. And he said that he would, in the morning, ask her father's consent to their engagement.

It so happened that on the very day that he told Rosa of his affection, and she had said frankly that she had loved him from the very first, that her father returned home in a more than usually good temper, and informed Kingston, who was just on the point of returning to his ship (which was to sail on the following day) that he wished to see him at his office in the morning, as he thought he should have " some pleasant news " for him.

"And I too wished to see you, sir, to-morrow morning," said Kingston, as he bade his host good-bye, and went off, wildly elated.

At eleven o'clock he found his employer in his office. He was smoking a cigar, and looked the personification of good humour and business contentment.

"Ha, here you are, Kingston. Sit down. Take a cigar. Just heard definitely about a certain matter. You have heard of the *Jalasco* brig?"

"Yes, sir, I have heard a good deal about her as one of the fastest brigs on the coast."

"Well, I've had my eye on her for a long time. Just the vessel for the Chiloe and Patagonian trade, new, well-armed, fast, and of good carrying capacity. Moreno Brothers, I knew, wanted to sell her, as they are in a tight place, but they wanted too much coin. However, to make a long story short, I made them an offer for her some weeks ago—thirty thousand dollars— and this morning Diego Moreno came and

accepted it. And you are to have command
of her. Riecke" (Kingston's chief mate)
"shall have the *Rosa*. The *Jalasco* is on
her way down from Callao now, and ought
to be here in a few weeks ; so you can wait
for her, and I'll send the *Rosa* to sea.
Hope you're satisfied ?"

"Indeed I am, sir," said Kingston grate-
fully; "she is a beautiful vessel; and
though I am sorry in one way to leave the
Rosa, I shall be proud to command her;"
and then without further ado, and thinking
it a fitting moment, he bluntly told his
employer of his love for Rosa, and asked his
consent to their engagement.

Captain Forestier heard him in silence,
then he rose from his seat, and Kingston
saw that his face was set, stern, and cold.
In a few brief moments the young captain's
hopes of Rosa's father giving his consent to
their union were dashed to the ground.

"I thought," said the old man slowly, as
he bent over towards Kingston, and almost

scowled at him from under his thick, bushy eyebrows, " that you were a man whom I could trust. I have done much to advance you. You have returned my confidence in you by ensnaring the affections of my daughter in an underhand and clandestine manner. You are a dishonourable scoundrel, and from this moment are no longer in my employ. Attempt to see my daughter again at your peril. . . . Stop !" and he raised his clenched hand passionately; " I will hear no excuses; your conduct admits of none. I will thank you to at once remove your effects from the brigantine. My cashier will pay you whatever is due to you."

Then stepping to the door that opened into the main office, he called the cashier.

" Mr Thompson, Captain Kingston has left my service. Pay him whatever is due, together with three months' extra pay as well."

Too stunned to attempt to make any

further protest, yet burning with mingled shame and anger, Kingston followed the sympathising cashier into the outer office, drew what money he was entitled to, but refused to accept the extra three months' pay.

Then he went to his friend the English storekeeper, and sat down and wrote a long letter to Rosa, telling her all that had occurred, and saying he would never give her up.

"I shall leave here to-morrow, dearest," he concluded, "for Callao, where I am in great hopes of getting a berth in one of Lorimer's vessels trading along the coast. But I shall have to begin as second mate again, I fear. Let us hope that your father will receive me differently when I ask him for you again. If he does not—well, then I shall take you.

"I tried to tell him that I would never have met you if I had known that he had such a strong objection to me as a future

son-in-law, but he would not listen to me;
and, fearful of further angering him, I
submitted in silence; and really, Rosa,
when those fierce blue eyes of his looked
I half felt that I *had* done something
underhanded, and also that I was a
blundering donkey to so placidly believe
that because *you* loved me, your father
was bound to like me and that there was
nothing but plain sailing before me."

He sent the letter to Rosa by a messenger,
and the same evening received a hurriedly
written answer, full of the tenderest love
and devotion, and saying, as lovers in-
variably do say, that she would always be
true to him, no matter what might befall;
that her father was terribly incensed, but
that her mother and sisters thought with
her that he would come round in time.
"And," she added, "although he stormed
at me dreadfully, he did not think of
telling me that I must not write to you,
but he is sure to do so; so I am *now*, this

very moment, making you a promise that
I shall write to you, wherever you may be.
So you see, dear, that when·he tells me
I must not write I can truthfully say that
I promised you I should. I can be just
as firm as he is, dear old man. But oh,
I wish he were not so unjust to you; it
makes me very unhappy, for he is. the
dearest father in all the world. We must
be patient, dearest, and hope."

The good-natured storekeeper, in whom
he felt safe in confiding as a reliable and
trustworthy man, willingly consented to
be the means of communication between
himself and Rosa, and cheered him up by
saying that although old Forestier was of
an exceedingly dictatorial and overbearing
nature, he was yet too fond of his children
to long stand in the way of the happiness
of any one of them.

On the following day, Kingston bade
his former landlord good-bye, and took
passage in a small Spanish vessel, bound

to Arica, from where he was pretty sure of getting to Callao. But in this expectation he was disappointed when he reached Arica, and was told that he might have to wait a month or more before any vessel would leave Arica for that port. However, he had no choice but to wait, so resigned himself to the inevitable.

He took up his quarters at a house much frequented by the captains of English and American ships, and which was kept by an ex-American whaling captain, a man named Vigors, whose wife was a Spanish woman. It did not take him long to learn that both Vigors and his pretty little wife were engaged in smuggling operations, which were connived at by the port authorities, who shared in the proceeds.

Almost every day and night, Vigors was visited by numbers of ruffianly looking characters, with whom he would have long conversations in private. They all, of

course, Vigors included, spoke in Spanish,
and did not seem to care whether Kingston, who, Vigors knew, understood that
language, overheard them or not. However, as they were always perfectly civil
to him, and Vigors himself tried to make
him as comfortable as he could in his so-
called hotel, he endured their presence in
the evening with patience. In the day-
time he contrived to pass the time fairly
well, making excursions into the country
through the fertile Azape Valley, returning at dusk to the Hotel La Serena, as
Vigors's establishment was called. Sometimes the host, when he was not engaged
with his smuggling friends, would play a
game of cards with him for moderate
stakes; and on one occasion, when Kingston
had lost, and handed a gold coin to Vigors,
the latter frankly advised him not to
display his money too freely in Arica,
especially in his house.

"These friends of mine you see here are

a pretty tough lot, and the sight of gold would be a bit too much for them. And I guess I don't want anything to happen to you through any fault of mine."

Kingston thanked him for his candour, said he would be careful, and from that time began to like the man.

One evening, on his return from his usual ride into the country, he found that Vigors had a visitor, a big florid-faced man whom he introduced as Captain Rowley, and who had, he said, just arrived from Callao in a coasting vessel. He and Vigors were evidently old acquaintances, and the habitués of the house also seemed to know the newcomer very well, for he addressed nearly all of them by their Christian names, and was very liberal to them in the way of refreshments. He seemed pleased, 'as a brother Englishman,' to make Kingston's acquaintance; and before half an hour had passed the two were on friendly terms, telling each other of their seafaring experiences in various parts of the world. Rowley seemed much interested when he learned that Kingston knew the South Sea Islands and the China Seas pretty well—having been second mate of a Hobart Town whaler for several cruises, as well as having had many years' experience in trading vessels.

"And so you're going to Valparaiso to look for another ship ? " he said meditatively, after Kingston had told him pretty well all his story—for he somehow felt attracted to the big, voluble, red-faced captain. "There's not much in that, is there? I know the Lorimers—a mean lot, I can tell you. Forestier isn't any better, or he wouldn't have served you as he did. Why, does he think he's going to marry the girl to a Prince of the blood royal? It was a dirty kick-out for you, I must say."

"It was," said the young man, his face flushing with anger as he thought of the old merchant's insults.

"Now look here," said Rowley, with sudden confidence; "you chuck up this idea of going to Callao. There's nothing in it, and it'll take you a month of Sundays to make any money. Come with me. You're just the man I want. You know the South Seas and the China coast; I don't, and neither does my mate. I'll give you rattling good money if you'll do second mate's duty, and help us in the navigating work; for, to tell you the truth, neither Merrill—that's my mate—nor myself are good navigators, though we're right enough along the coast."

"Where is your ship?" asked Kingston in surprise.

"Not far off by this time," replied Rowley, with a laugh. "Now look here, I'll tell you the whole truth. I've got a fine brig, and I've been making a pretty penny in the contraband line between Panama and the southern ports, but when I was ashore in Callao a few weeks ago a friend of mine there told me that my brig was to be seized within a few days, and that I was being watched. He helped me to get away into the country that night, and took a letter from me off to my mate telling him to slip his cable and skip, and pick me up at Arica. I'm safe enough here, as I'm among friends, and I expect Merrill every day now. He won't come to an anchor, but there's a couple of men on the top of the morro on the look-out for him day and night; and Vigors has a boat ready to put me aboard. Now what do you say?"

"First of all I want to know where you are bound to?"

"China. I'm sick of this trade; it's too risky, though there's a lot of money in it. The brig is well armed, and just the right sort of ship for the opium trade."

"I don't particularly care about leaving South America," said Kingston, who was thinking of Rosa.

"No, I daresay not. But look here," and Rowley bent forward with an eager

4

light in his staring blue eyes, "I want you
badly—that's the truth. Now, I'll tell you
what I'll do. If you will see us safe into
Macao harbour, I'll give you two thousand
dollars."

"You *must* have made money," said
Kingston, with a laugh.

"I've done pretty well, pretty well, and
mean to do better. Now, is it a deal?"

"Yes, I can't resist such a good offer.
Two thousand dollars means a lot to a poor
man like me."

"Come here, Jimmy, my buck," cried
Rowley, gleefully, to Vigors, "bring us some
writing gear. Mr. Kingston here and me
are doing a bit of business."

Vigors brought writing materials, and in
a few minutes Kingston had signed an
agreement to navigate the brig *Blossom*
to Macao for two thousand dollars, and
Rowley paid one quarter of the sum down
in gold.

That night he wrote a long hopeful letter

to Rosa, telling her of his good fortune, and saying that with two thousand dollars added to what he had previously saved, he would at least be able to buy a share in a small vessel on the South American coast, and all going well, he would be back in Valparaiso within twelve months. The letter with the money he confided to the care of Vigors— whom he felt he could trust—to send to the care of his friend the storekeeper in Valparaiso.

Two or three days after he had signed the agreement with Rowley, the latter suddenly left Vigors's establishment. He took with him eight or ten of Vigors's smuggling friends; they were all armed and mounted, and Kingston saw the party ride off in the direction of Azape Valley.

On joining Vigors and his wife at breakfast, he found a note from Rowley, telling him to hold himself in readiness, as all going well, he (Rowley) expected that the brig would be off Arica that or the following night, and that Vigors would have a boat in readiness to convey him on board.

"Why could not he wait here till the brig was off the port?" asked Kingston, naturally enough, of Vigors.

The American shook his head, and said that that would not do—the authorities of Arica, although they were actually concerned in many of his and Rowley's transactions, dared not wink at his openly leaving the country under their very eyes, when a price was offered for his apprehension, and the Government had given orders for the seizure of the brig. Therefore, he added, Rowley had gone off with his party along the coast to a rendezvous arranged with Merrill, where the old crew, of whose trustworthiness he was not assured, were to be put ashore and the men who had ridden away with him put in their places.

This sounded reasonable enough, and Kingston was quite satisfied, when, after his usual game of cards with his host, he turned

in. It was then about midnight, and the
night being cool, he was soon asleep. He
had, however, not slumbered for more than
an hour, when he was awakened by the
sound of galloping hoofs along the dusty
road. They stopped at the courtyard of
Vigors's house, and presently he heard the
American and his wife talking to someone
in the adjoining room ; a few minutes later,
Vigors came to his room and called to him
to dress.

"Hurry up, Mr. Kingston. Rowley's ship
is lying-to outside. The boat is all ready."

Dressing himself as quickly as possible,
and pitching his few belongings into a bag,
he went into the other room, where Vigors
was awaiting him. Bidding Senora Vigors
a warm good-bye, he followed his host along
the deserted sea front to the waterside, where
a boat, manned by two men, was lying.
They passed close beside the guardship lying
in the centre of the port, without being
challenged, and rounding the northern arm

of the harbour, saw the brig lying-to about
a mile away under the dark shadow of the
beetling morro. No lights were visible on
board. Taking up a lighted lantern, which
was standing in the bottom of the boat,
partly covered by a coat, Vigors held it aloft
for an instant.

"She sees us," he said as the brig, in
response to the signal, at once filled and
stood towards the boat; "pull, Miguel; pull,
Pedro."

The boat was soon alongside, and Vigors
and Kingston clambered on deck, where
they were met by Rowley and his mate,
who shook hands with them.

"Ha, Mr. Kingston, welcome on board the
Blossom," said the big captain effusively.
"Now, will you please come on the poop
with me, and take charge of the ship, as my
mate and myself have to transact a little
business with our good friend Vigors before
he goes ashore. I'll call the hands aft first,
however, before I go below and 'talk

some' to 'em, as my mate would say. Just
to introduce 'em to you," and he laughed
boisterously.

"Come aft, men," he bawled in English.
"I want to speak to you for a minute.
Show a leg, you yellow-hided Dagoes."

The crew trooped aft, and then Rowley
addressed them vigorously in Spanish, telling
them that the man who stood beside him
was not only a personal friend of his and a
gentleman, but their new second mate as
well; and also that he (Kingston) was able
and willing to knock "the eyeballs out of
anyone, or the whole lot of them, if they
didn't move along slippy." Then he wound
up by telling them that he (Rowley) had no
doubt that Senor Kingston, to show his
good-will towards his new shipmates, would
allow both watches to drink his health in
good French cognac, and that the steward
would bring them half a dozen bottles up
presently.

The 'yellow-hided Dagoes' viva'd both

el Capitan Rowley and Senor Kingston most
enthusiastically ; and Rowley, who seemed
to be in most exuberant spirits, again shook
hands with his new second mate and went
below, leaving Kingston in charge.

The steward brought up the bottles of
brandy, and in a few minutes the entire
crew gathered around the fore-hatch and
about the windlass, and Kingston heard
them laughing and talking as they opened
the bottles and drank each other's health,
and those of the captain, Senor Merrill, and
Senor Kingston.

Presently a huge American negro who
was standing beside the helmsman came up
to the new officer and saluted.

"Good ebening, sah. I'se de bo'sun,
sah, Shall I go for'ard, sah, an' see dat
dose fellows don' kick up too much
bobbery ? "

"Just as you please, bo'sun," replied
Kingston, with a smile at the word
'bobbery,' which brought old memories

of East India 'country ships' to his mind.

The business which Vigors had to transact with Captain Rowley and his mate did not take long to complete, for in less than a quarter of an hour the three came on deck together, all evidently in high spirits.

" Good-bye, Mr. Kingston. I wish you all good luck," said Vigors, warmly shaking the new officer's hand. " Good-bye, Ben; good-bye, Tom;" and with two very large and heavy bags of dollars he went over the side into his boat, which at once pushed off and pulled shoreward. Then Rowley and Merrill again went below.

As Kingston paced to and fro on the poop, he became aware of a fact that, when he first stepped on board, he had not noticed—the decks had been washed down, and were not yet dry. No rain, he knew, could have fallen at that time of the year, and it was a strange thing to wash decks late at night.

Presently, as he passed the skylight, he glanced down and saw that Rowley and Merrill were engaged in the agreeable task of counting money. Quite one half of the cabin table was covered with bags of silver coin, piled three or four deep, while the contents of five or six bags lay in a loose heap before Merrill, who was refilling the bags from which they had been emptied. Rowley had before him long rows of gold in piles, the amount of which, as he counted, he called out to Merrill, and then entered on a slip of paper.

"Very pleasant occupation," thought Kingston, as he turned away somewhat enviously; "smuggling must be a very lucrative business. If I had one-twentieth part of that money, I would drop sailorising pretty quickly."

He walked to the fife rail, and leaning across it, looking for'ard, placing one foot on the edge of the waterway. Then he felt something soft against the toe of his boot.

He stooped and touched it, and then shuddered.

It was a severed hand, clinging with its dead, cold fingers to one of the iron stanchions of the fife rail. On the middle finger was a ring, set with a large moonstone, which glowed and shone under the starlight.

The hand had been cut off about two inches above the wrist, evidently by a stroke of sword or cutlass from above; and in an instant Kingston realised that some bloody tragedy had occurred on the *Blossom* less than an hour before, for ensanguined drops were still falling from the wrist upon the deck below.

He sprang to the skylight, and looked down.

"Come on deck, Captain Rowley," he cried, "and tell me what sort of a craft is this, where dead men's hands are lying around!"

CHAPTER IV.

As Kingston's angry call rang out, the negro boatswain rushed aft, and sprang up the poop ladder just as Rowley, red-faced and flustered, appeared from the cabin. Merrill came after him in a leisurely manner, cigar in mouth, and looking perfectly calm and undisturbed.

"What is the matter, Mr. Kingston?" said Rowley. "What has upset you?"

"'Upset' me, man!" cried Kingston sternly, and striding forward he placed his hand on the captain's shoulder and almost pushed him to the fife rail. "What the blazes does that mean?" and he pointed to the severed hand clasping the stanchion, on which the iridiscent gem still shone brightly; "what bloody work has been going on here to-night?"

Merrill shot the captain a swift glance, commanding silence; then stooping down, he unbent the stiffened fingers of the dead hand, and in another instant had thrown it far overboard.

"Lay aft, some of you, and give the poop a better wash down," he cried out sharply to the crew. "Away for'ard, bo'sun! You, Captain Rowley, and you, Mr. Kingston, go below. I guess I'll take charge of this hooker for a few minutes;" and he looked so threateningly at the captain that the latter, clutching Kingston's arm, hurried him below.

"Sit down, Mr. Kingston, sit down," he said pantingly; "I can explain everything presently——"

Merrill put his head down through the skylight. "Put a stopper your jaw-tackle until *I* come down, Ben," he said nonchalantly. "I guess that Mr. Kingston can wait a few minutes. But, at the same time, so as to save you from coming on deck again just now, Mr. Kingston, will you kindly give us a course?"

"You shall get no course, nor anything else from me, until I know what sort of ship this is," replied Kingston, looking up.

Merrill smiled and nodded, and then in another moment they heard his voice speaking to the man at the wheel.

"West by north, Antonio."

"Wes' by nor', senor," responded Antonio in English.

Then, as Merrill paced to and fro in the poop and the crew scrubbed it down a second time, Rowley and Kingston sat facing each other, listening and waiting.

"You can come aft now, bo'sun," called out Merrill after a few minutes. "I'm going below for a while."

"Aye, aye, sah," replied the negro in his deep tones as he obeyed the order, and

the mate drew him aside out of hearing
and spoke rapidly to him in whispered
tones.

Then Merrill stepped into the cabin, cool
and self-possessed, and took a seat at the
table.

"Now, Ben," he said, as he took off his
cap, laid it on a chair, and lighted a fresh
cigar, "I guess that you had better just sit
quiet and let *me* tell Mr. Kingston what has
occurred—you look too flushed to do anything more than take a drink."

Rowley eagerly assented to the suggestion,
and hurriedly rising he went to the sideboard and brought a decanter of brandy,
some water and glasses. Merrill poured
him out half a tumberful of brandy and
placed it before him, then with an
unmoved face passed the decanter to
Kingston and politely asked him to help
himself.

"Thank you," said the new officer, rather
coldly, as he poured out a very little and

returned the decanter to Merrill, who helped himself more liberally.

" Now, Mr. Kingston," began the mate, as, after drinking his liquor, he leant back in his chair, " we did have a rather nasty muss on board, and of course meant to have told you all about it as soon as Vigors had gone. The fact is, our old crew did not like turning out of the ship, and before the captain and I could interfere, they and the new crew were at it hammer and tongs, with knives, pistols and hatchets. Then matters began to get pretty serious, I can tell you; for a dozen of them made a rush aft, and in trying to beat them back the captain got a graze from a bullet on his left arm, and a crack on the head at the same time which stunned him."

Rowley opened his coat, and Kingston saw that his arm was bandaged under the coat sleeve.

" Oh it's nothing, nothing to speak of," he said nervously. " A man must expect

this sort of thing sometimes on this coast
and in such a business."

"Well," resumed Merrill, "the moment
the skipper fell, matters became worse, for
in an instant some of the old crew shouted
out that they would either take the ship
or some of the money which they knew was
in the cabin—Ben's and my hard earnings.
I had to let the captain lie where he fell,
and help to keep the poop from being
rushed ; and I can tell you, sir, that I found
these little things come in mighty handy,"
and putting his hand in his coat pocket he
took out a pair of brass knuckle-dusters. " I
daren't use my pistol for fear of shooting
some of our own men who had been dragged
down off the poop and were being half-
murdered by the fellows on the main deck.
Then it was that I saw one of our men who
was standing near me make a slash with his
cutlass at a man who was trying to climb
up through the fife rail stanchions, and I
heard him yell out that his hand was cut
5

off. Well, that about finished the row, for the old crew had had enough, and I guess some of them were pretty badly hurt."

"Did you manage to get clear of them all?" asked Kingston, who now began to feel a certain amount of sympathy for the two men.

"All but four, who sided with us," put in Rowley, "so I've kept them; the others, with the chap who lost his hand, we put ashore about ten miles up the coast."

There was nothing very surprising in Rowley's story, nor in the summary manner in which he had got rid of his former crew. In those days the West Coast of South America was a rough place, and the use of knife and pistol, even on an ordinary merchant vessel, was regarded as a perfectly proper and legitimate manner of settling either private disputes or breaches of discipline,

"Well, there was a darned unpleasant mess to clean up, Mr. Kingston," went on Merrill, "but how on earth that poor devil's hand was left there clutching the stanchion I don't know. Guess if it had not been for that ring it would not have been noticed until daylight to-morrow. Anyway, Mister Diego Miranda is just as well without his right hand—I know he's cut a good many throats with it in his time, and he was bent on cutting more."

After some further conversation, Kingston went on deck again, Merrill arranging to take the morning watch. The brig was slipping through the water very quickly, for the sea was smooth, and she was now under all sail except stun' sails. The watch were lounging about on the main deck, and only the boatswain was on the poop, standing beside the helmsman. He touched his hat to the new officer and made some remark upon the fineness of the night, to which Kingston replied, and then walked over to the lee side. Then, for the first time, the officer noticed that the negro had his head bandaged.

"Did you get hurt too, bo'sun?" he inquired.

"Yes, sah. Got a nasty cut on de top of de brain box," the man replied, with a laugh that showed his white teeth.

"Well, it might have been worse."

"Yes, sah. Dat's so. Dere was in a consider'ble muss, dere was. We had a mighty tough job to shift dose, dose—de ole crew, sah."

Kingston made no more inquiries. It was no concern of his, he thought, as he paced to and fro—the affair was over, and he would ask no further questions about it. Rowley and his men were evidently a rough lot, but that did not matter to him as long as he was treated as his position demanded, and so far he had nothing to complain about, and all going well, he might stay on a bit longer with

Rowley in the brig after they reached
Macao. Then his thoughts went back to
Rosa Forestier.

When he was relieved by Merrill, he
went below to a very comfortable cabin,
and in a few minutes was sound asleep.

During the following week, everything
went on very smoothly. The brig was
remarkably fast, and as the wind continued
very steady, she made excellent progress.
Merrill, too, knew how to make the best
of her, though Rowley, greatly to Kingston's surprise, seemed almost a stranger
to his own ship—did not seem to even
know which was her best sailing point;
and, furthermore, though he endeavoured
to conceal the fact from his new second
mate, certainly did not know what stores
and spare sails and other gear were on
board, until he saw them overhauled
personally. Then, too, Kingston found
that instead of he and Merrill being merely
poor navigators, as Rowley had told him

in Arica, they possessed scarcely any
knowledge of navigation at all! As for
their seamanship, however, no fault could
be found with that, and they certainly
had an obedient, if an ill-looking and
lazy crew, and it was easy to see that
Rowley, with all his bluff good-humour,
was not a man to be trifled with.

Day after day passed under the same
unvarying conditions of weather—a sky
of blue, flecked now and then by a few
fleecy clouds, a bright, warm sun by day
and a star-studded heaven by night, and
a steady generous breeze which sped the
brig swiftly along till a long low line of
trees, that seemed to rise from the sea
itself, showed on the horizon right ahead;
and Kingston, coming down from the fore-
yard, told the captain that the line of trees
fringed the sandy shores of a great lagoon,
encompassed by a belt of roaring surf, and
that it was the eastern outlier of the little-
known but wide spread archipelago known

as the Paumotu Group, with many of the
islands of which he was familiar.

" We shall have to keep a sharp look-
out at night now," he said; "most of the
Paumotu islands are very low, and we
shall need to be careful."

And a careful watch was kept, two men
always being on the look-out at night,
one being stationed on the fore yard, the
other on the topgallant foc'sc'le, but even
then Kingston was somewhat nervous,
for with the exception of the negro boatswain, there was not a man among the
crew whom he could trust. They were
all to a man lazy, useless fellows, and the
poorest seamen he had ever sailed with.
Worcester, the boatswain, on the other
hand, was not only a splendid seaman,
but a very intelligent man. He had served
for four years on the British frigate *Blonde*,
so he one day told Kingston, but in con-
sequence of an undeserved affront put
upon him by one of the officers, had

deserted at Panama, where he had met and taken service with Rowley. Of either Rowley's or Merrill's antecedents, however, he would say nothing, and plainly evinced his disinclination to answer any of Kingston's most guarded inquiries. Generally a good tempered man, when not interfered with, he was liable to sudden and dangerous outbursts of passion, and even Rowley and Merrill, both men of the most determined courage, addressed him as their equal. His enormous stature and tremendous strength afforded a startling contrast to the slender, undersized Chileno and Mexican seamen, for whom he had the most supreme contempt as 'sogers,' and they, in return, hated him most fervently, though were too cowardly to show it.

There was, however, another person on board beside Worcester, whom Kingston rather liked. This was the steward, a young and extremely good-looking Peruvian named José Pimental, who had formerly been one of Vigors's most trusted associates. He was always particularly civil and obliging to the new officer, and did much to make him comfortable when it was his watch below.

CHAPTER V.

FOR the following three or four days the brig ran steadily before the south-east trades, which were accompanied by continuous rain, and Kingston passed an anxious time, for they were now in the centre of the vast cluster of islands comprising the Paumotu group, which being continuously sighted on all sides, the utmost care was needed.

One night as he lay smoking in his bunk, unable to sleep, and waiting till his watch was called, he noticed a pile of books and newspapers on a shelf in his cabin. They had evidently been left there as valueless by the former occupant of the cabin, and hitherto he had had no time to look at the collection and see if there was anything among them worth reading. He rose and took them down one by one, and then uttered an exclamation of surprise when on the fly-leaf of one he saw written, "Thomas Merrill, Brig. *Jalasco*," and on several of the newspapers, which were New York publications, he saw the same name with the address "Brig *Jalasco*, care of the Moreno Brothers, Callao."

"This is very curious," he thought. "Merrill, as well as Rowley, has heard me talking of the *Jalasco* often enough, but has never even said that he knew her! Perhaps, however, he had to leave her for a reason that he does not care to talk about. And he certainly is not a very communicative man."

He sat down, book in hand, and began to read. The brig was travelling at a great rate through the water, though under easy canvas, and he could hear the slat of heavy driving rain on the sides of the skylight overhead.

"I hope those greasers are keeping a good lookout," he said aloud to himself, and then almost at the same moment he heard Merrill's voice cry out sharply—

"Hard down, hard down! Let go fore and main——"

The rest of the order he did not hear, for ere he was half-way out of the cabin, the brig struck with a crash, and then heeled over on her broadside, where she lay for a moment till a heavy sea caught her and lifted her further on to the reef on which she had struck.

In an instant the wildest confusion prevailed, the Mexican and Chileno sailors at once becoming terrified, and paying no attention to the orders shouted by the officers. Rowley had sprung on deck at the same time as Kingston, and through the fierce driving rain they saw that the brig was lying in a white seeth of foam, and could hear her grinding and crushing the coral on which she rested. Then in quick succession

three long combers came sweeping up astern
and drove her, bumping, tearing, and shaking in every timber, further on across the
reef, just as the boatswain cried out that he
could see smooth water ahead.

" Let her drive, sir !   Let her drive if she
will," shouted Kingston to the captain, who
was bawling to the crew to let go everything;
" give her all the lifting canvas we can, and
she'll drag over ;"   and then as another
mountain sea loomed up through the mist
astern, he cried out for everyone to take to
the rigging, and thrusting aside the terrified
Chileno who was at the wheel, he and the
negro boatswain grasped the spokes.

On came the grim, grey wall of water,
curling over and breaking with a dull roar
on the edge of the reef ; and then, lifting the
brig on its hissing foam, it carried her, aided
by the wind, clear across the reef into the
smooth water on the other side, her stern
post and rudder actually breaking off a portion of the inside edge of the coral barrier,

as she ploughed into the deeper water beyond.

Hitting and kicking the cowardly crew off the poop, Rowley and his officers drove them to the braces, and in a few minutes the brig was brought-to under the lee of the reef in five fathoms; and after being given thirty fathoms of chain, lay quietly to her anchor in smooth water, though the wind was blowing strongly, and there was a wild sea beating on the reef.

" That was a narrow squeak," said Kingston to the captain, as the men came down from aloft; "had she struck at low water, she would have been matchwood by now. Is she making any water, bo'sun ? "

" Very little as yet, sah ; de pumps sucked in five minutes, and de water is very dirty."

Rowley gave a sigh of relief, for he had feared that the brig had sustained serious damage when she first crashed into the reef. Then he motioned to Kingston to follow him below, where he thanked him

earnestly for his presence of mind in acting
as he did.

"Only for you advising me to let her
drag on, I should have no ship now," he
said, extending his hand.

Kingston, sailor-like, made a light answer,
and turned the conversation into another
channel by expressing a wish for daylight,
so that they could see where they were; for,
as he said, the brig might have run into a
lagoon from which there was no exit for a
vessel of her draught—there were many
such places in the Paumotu group. Then
he went on deck again, and busied himself
in attending to various matters.

Before daylight the wind fell, and the sky
cleared; and when the mounting sun had
dispelled the haze which over hung the
lagoon, he and the captain, to their delight,
saw that the brig was in an atoll of about
four miles in length by two in width, and
that on the opposite, or western side, there
was a clear and apparently deep passage

between two islets thickly covered with coco-palms. No signs of inhabitants could be discerned on any of the eight or ten islets which, connected by the reef, enclosed the lagoon.

"We are all right as far as getting out again goes, captain. It would be a pretty bad thing for us if there were no passage out of this circle of land. Seven years ago, when I was in the Caroline Islands, I saw a fine, big and new Liverpool ship lying abandoned in Namorek Lagoon. She had done exactly what we did—struck the reef at high tide on a dark night, bumped over it into smooth water, and brought up in a mill pond, completely enclosed by a circular reef. She never got out again, and had to be abandoned by the captain and crew. The natives had some fine pickings, I can assure you."

Against this pleasurable discovery of an exit from the lagoon, however, was the fact that Merrill reported that the ship was now making water pretty freely, and would require half an hour's steady pumping in every watch. To a suggestion from Kingston that they should make for Tahiti, where the brig could be examined by native divers, and, if necessary, beached for repairs, Rowley gave such a nervous and yet strenuous negative, saying it would cause them too much loss of time, that the second officer dropped the subject.

So, early that afternoon the anchor was lifted, and the brig sailed out safely through the western passage, and continued on her course till the great lagoon island of Hao, one of the Paūmotu Archipelago, was sighted three days later.

Shortly after breakfast, Kingston went aloft, as he wished to get a better view of the land. He had scarcely seated himself on the fore-yard when he heard the sound of a violent altercation on deck, and looking down, saw the boatswain struggling with two of the Mexican seamen, both of whom

6

had drawn their knives. Both Merrill and the captain were below at the time, so he at once went to the negro's assistance, just in time to prevent the rest of the crew from joining their shipmates in the attack on the boatswain, who had already stretched one of his assailants senseless on the deck, and had seized the other by the back of his neck in a grip of iron.

"Come aft, you lazy soger, an' see what de captain has to say 'bout dis," cried Worcester, pushing the man, who still grasped his knife, before him, and followed by Kingston, who saw that mischief was brewing. The three came to the break of the poop just as Rowley ran up from his cabin and asked what was the matter.

As he spoke, the rest of the crew, their knives out, made a sudden rush to try and liberate their shipmate from the negro, but Kingston, whipping out a belaying pin from the rail, threatened to knock down the first man who tried to interfere, and

they at once drew back. Then the boatswain, still keeping his grip on the man,
addressed the captain in a voice thick with
rage, and said that while he was for'ard, he
had overheard Antonio (the man he then
held) tell another that he (Antonio) had
been put on the look-out the night the brig
had struck, but had deserted his post, and
gone into the galley to be out of the rain.

"Let him go," said the captain, curtly.

"Let him go, sah !" the negro repeated
indignantly ; "why, sah, I thought you'd
kick him along de deck till yo' was tired.
And den he an' his mate Matto drew der
knives on me."

"That is true," said Kingston, coming
forward. "I was aloft and saw the pair of
them rush at the boatswain with their
knives."

Rowley shot a quick glance at the
crew, who were grouped on the main
deck, and then again ordered the boatswain
to let the man go, and it was evident

to Kingston that he feared to incur their resentment.

"But he drew his knife on me, sah," again protested the negro, "an' he'll put it into my back de fust chance he gets. I don' trust a mongrel like dat."

"Bah!" said the captain, contemptuously, "don't be such a cur. Let him go, I tell you."

The negro's lips twitched convulsively, and for the moment he was unable to speak, and seemed as if he were choking with the violence of the passion that filled his mighty bosom. Then suddenly drawing the wretched Antonio towards him with his right hand, he struck him with the left on the arm with such terrific force, that the bone snapped like a carrot, and the knife fell upon the deck, and he then threw him clean across the deck, against the bulwarks on the port side, were he lay like a dead man, doubled up in a heap.

"Dat's fo' de man, brack, white or yaller;

" ' Stand back ! ' "

[*See page* 85.

dat draws a knife on John Worcester," he said in a voice thick and guttural with fury; and, ere Kingston could stay him, he sprang up the poop ladder and faced Rowley; "an' de man dat says I'm a cur is a liar; an' if he don' take it back, I'se goin' to ram de lie down his throat."

"Stand back!" cried Merrill, springing to the captain's side, and pointing a pistol at the negro's head. In an instant Worcester tore it from his grasp, and hurled it overboard—only to find another presented at him by Rowley, whose hand, as he pulled the trigger, was knocked up by Kingston, and the bullet sped into the air.

"Shame, Captain Rowley!" he cried, thrusting him back, "shame! Would you murder an unarmed man?" and then as the crew again made a rush aft, to get at Worcester, he sprang to meet them.

"Back, you dogs! I'll kill the first man that puts foot on this poop, if he attempts to touch the boatswain!"

There was a dead silence. Rowley, empty pistol in hand, and face flushed purple, was looking at the negro, who stood before him with folded arms with such dignity and sudden self-restraint that even Merrill eyed him in silent admiration.

"Yo' would have killed me, captain, yo' would. But fo'all dat, sah, I'se a man . . . . an' I'll let it all pass if you take dose words back."

"I take them back, bo'sun," said Rowley sullenly.

The negro touched his cap, and without a word turned away, and descended to the main deck. For a moment he stood looking at the crew, who were slinking for'ard; then in a voice that was utterly devoid of temper, he called out—

"Take a pull on de lee fore brace dere, some of you."

The watch obeyed him sullenly, and then Merrill and Kingston brought Antonio into the cabin, and set his arm, neither of them making the slightest allusion to the fracas, and Rowley, who watched the operation, did so in silence, and by tacit consent the matter was not again discussed by any one.

Worcester went about his duties as usual, but he took occasion that night to grasp Kingston's hand and mutter his gratitude, and the officer whispered to him to be on his guard with the crew. The negro nodded—he could do no more, for the man at the wheel was evidently listening.

One day when the brig was almost clear of the Paumotu group, a low sandy islet, covered with short, thick *toa*[1] trees was sighted, and as the brig was short of fuel, Rowley hove-to, and with Kingston and two seamen, went ashore to cut firewood. The landing was somewhat dangerous, on account of the surf running on the reef;

[1] *Toa* is a species of casuarina which grows very plentifully on most of the coral atolls of the North and South Pacific.

the boat, too, was heavy, clumsily-built,
and steered with a rudder, which latter,
Kingston saw, would be useless in a swiftly
running and breaking sea, especially when
there were but two men to pull. However,
the captain was determined to land, but
allowed the second officer to take an oar.

After lying on their oars for a few
minutes outside the belt of surf, watching
for a favourable opportunity, Rowley gave
the word, and under the three oars the
boat was headed for the reef.

"Bend to it, men, bend to it!" cried
Kingston, who, looking astern, could see
an ugly-looking green sea with combing
top, that threatened to break before the
boat was over the edge of the reef. The
seamen responded to his call all they could,
but just as the boat was within a few feet
of the coral barrier, the backwash from a
preceding roller poured down its face like
an avalanche, and Rowley, with one look at
the towering sea astern, foolishly gave the

order to back water, with disastrous
consequences, for as the boat lay deep in
the foaming trough right under the edge
of the reef, the mighty wall of incoming
water fell on her with a thundering crash,
and rolled her over and over.

As soon as he came to the surface,
Kingston, who was a powerful swimmer,
shook the water from his eyes and in-
stinctively swam out away from the reef.
Looking back he saw that the boat was
badly stove, and had been carried ashore,
and the two seamen with her, for he could
just see their heads and shoulders as they
stood up in the shallow water covering
the reef.

"Where is the captain?" he shouted.

They threw up their hands, which meant
either that they did not know, or that
Rowley had disappeared; and neither of
them made any effort to come to the
officer's assistance.

Raising his head as high as he could as

he swam, Kingston shouted again and again
in the hope that the captain, who was but
a poor swimmer, was somewhere near him;
and then as the backwash again poured
down the reef and left it bare, he caught
sight of Rowley clinging to a jagged edge
of exposed coral rock with the blood
streaming down his face in torrents.
Shouting encouragement to him, he swam
to his aid and reached him just as a sea
went over his head, for the unfortunate
man clung tenaciously to the rock as his
last hope of life, as the blood which poured
from a deep wound in his head had completely blinded him.

"I'm done, done," he gasped, as the
water sank down from the rock, and he
gained his breath again.

"Not a bit of it," cried Kingston; "quick,
hold on with one hand while I get off
your coat;" and before another sea reached
them, he had managed to free first the
captain's left, then his right arm from his

heavy pilot coat, shouting the while to the seamen to throw them an oar or a line from the edge of the reef. But there was no response to his cries — they were too afraid to venture out again, for fear of being swept away by the backwash.

"Let go now, and swim," he cried. "I will keep you up; we can't stay here."

Rowley obeyed, and, supported by Kingston, struck out seaward, away from the smothering surf, which would have soon exhausted him, and five minutes later they heard a loud cry from Worcester, who, with four hands, was quite near them with a second boat.

"Hurrah! Here they are, boys!"

The boat swept up, and both men were pulled in, Rowley so done up that he was almost unconscious. As quickly as possible he was taken on board, and carried below, where brandy was given him, and then Merrill sewed up the gaping wound in his head. In half an hour he was sufficiently recovered to sit up and thank his rescuers ; and acceded to Kingston's wish to allow him to go ashore again, and get at least one load of wood cut and brought off.

On this occasion the boatswain, who was used to surf work, accompanied the second officer, and the boat reached the beach safely. Here they found the two seamen, who after being vigorously cursed by Kingston for their cowardice, were given axes and set to work with the rest of the men. After an hour's labour, enough wood was cut and carried to the boat, but as the tide was now low, and the reef bare, the men were told to get their dinner and do what they pleased for the next few hours.

Then after eating a biscuit or two each, Kingston and the boatswain started off to have a look round the island, and see if they could discover some turtle eggs.

The moment they were well out of sight of the men, the negro placed his hand on his officer's arm, and said he had something important to confide to him—something that he had determined to tell him for many days past, but no opportunity had been given him.

"Let us sit down ober here, sah. I'se got a long story to tell you," he added.

They sat down, and the first words he uttered were sufficiently startling.

"I suppose, sah, you think dat dat brig is de *Blossom*?"

"Isn't she, then?" said Kingston in surprise.

"No, sah," replied the negro slowly, "dat is de *Jalasco*, and de skipper and Merrill pirated her de day before you come aboard. I had a hand in it myself. But I'se goin' to make a clean breast ob it, and if you want me to help you to capture an' carry de ship back again, I'll do it—dat is, if I ain't murdered before de time comes."

Then in as few words as possible, he told his story, which was grim enough.

When he met Rowley in Callao he

(Rowley) was without a ship, but taking
the negro into his confidence, told him that
he intended to seize a fine new brig which
was about to sail for Valparaiso, where she
was to be handed over to her new owners.
Merrill, who was second mate on board, was
to gain over some of the crew when near
Arica, seize the captain, mate, and rest of
the crew who would not join them, and
await Rowley, who would be expecting the
brig at an agreed-upon rendezvous. There
were on board over sixty thousand dollars
consigned to Moreno Brothers' Valparaiso
branch, and it was the money more than
anything else that tempted Rowley and
Merrill to the venture, though the vessel
herself would be a great prize, as she was
almost new, well-armed and found, and
could easily be sold in the East Indies or
China for a large sum of money, and no
unnecessary questions would be asked by
the purchasers.

Worcester consented to join, and through

Merrill's influence was shipped on the brig, and Rowley, who was well supplied with money, left Callao almost immediately in order to get to Arica, where he could easily, at the proper time, find a fresh crew among the smuggling fraternity who made Vigors's house their headquarters, and who had long been associated with him, Rowley, and even Merrill, in their daring ventures.

Merrill, so the boatswain said, was the real instigator of the enterprise. He and Rowley had known each other for many years and had had many desperate smuggling adventures together on the Venezuelan and Mexican coast. But once, during a hot pursuit of them by the guarda costas, they had to part, and did not meet again for over a twelvemonth.

Merrill, who was a man of the greatest daring and resource, had made his way to Callao, where he had succeeded in getting into the employment of Moreno Brothers as second mate of their new brig. Rowley was then in hiding in Panama, but Merrill wrote to him to come to Callao, as he thought they might do a good stroke of business.

At this time, however, he knew nothing of the intention of Moreno Brothers to sell the brig to Captain Forestier of Valparaiso, and had formed no definite plans beyond thinking that with Rowley's assistance it might be possible to quietly surprise the captain and chief mate when they were asleep and run off with the ship. But when he learnt that the vessel was sold, and, furthermore, that she would be conveying sixty thousand dollars to Valparaiso, he and Rowley set to work promptly and studied out their scheme in detail. The latter was possessed of, three or four thousand dollars, and some of this was used by Merrill in gaining over certain of the brig's crew—men whom they knew could be depended upon to assist them.

The brig did not sail for nearly a fortnight after the specie had been sent on board by

the owners, and thus Rowley had ample
time to get down the coast to Vigors.

Both the captain and mate of the brig
were Spaniards, but although rather careless regarding discipline, they were very
courageous men, and never for one moment
dreamt that there were traitors on board—
Merrill, Worcester, and five seamen.   All
went well till the brig was within a few
miles of the place where the attempt was to
be made, and where Rowley was to put in
an appearance.

"Dere's one thing, sah, dat I mus' say
'bout de skipper and Mr. Merrill. Dey did
not want to hab any bloodshed if dey could
help it; but dey was both powerful determined to get dose sixty thousand dollars.
An' dey just worked me up properly too,
an' I reckon I was just as keen on handling
my share ob de plunder—a thousand dollars
—as any one else ob de gang."

Merrill and Rowley had laid their plans
too elaborately for them to go astray, and

7

one day, towards dusk, the former told Worcester to keep a bright look-out for a light. The brig was then running down the coast, close in to the land, and only a light air filling her sails.

The Spanish captain, who was an extremely lazy and careless man, always turned in early, and both he and the mate were good sleepers.

"The moment we see the light, bo'sun, you know what you have to do. If the breeze should freshen up a bit all the better —we must haul up for the light, if we can, without making any noise. Captain Rowley has us in sight at this very moment, no doubt, and we want to have him alongside as quickly as we can."

An hour after the mate had turned in he was fast asleep, as Merrill could tell by his heavy breathing as he listened at his brother-officer's open door. Just as he walked softly on deck again, Worcester saw the expected light.

"Right," said Merrill. "Tell Antonio to keep her up to it as much as he can. It won't do for us to touch the braces. It might make too much noise. Now go for'ard."

Worcester stepped for'ard. All the men in the mate's watch (except two who were in Merrill's confidence and had purposely remained on deck) were sound asleep below, and the negro quickly secured the fore-scuttle.

Then Merrill and three of his fellow-conspirators, armed with cutlasses and pistols, went into the cabin, expecting to surprise the captain and mate fast asleep. It so happened, however, that the steward had been sitting in the companion way enjoying the cool night air, when he heard the fore-scuttle being secured, and at the same moment saw Merrill and those with him come softly along the deck with arms in their hands. In an instant he darted down below, and quickly awakened the captain and mate, just as Merrill and his party entered the cabin. Both the mate and captain met them, the former with a hatchet, and the latter with his pistols, and called on them to lay down their arms. Then, to his horror, Worcester, who was now in charge of the deck, heard a volley, and rushing down into the cabin, found the captain, mate, and steward weltering in their blood,—they had all been shot down remorselessly. Merrill at once assumed charge, and had just ordered the dying men to be taken on deck, when a sudden cry of alarm was given by the man at the wheel—the men confined for'ard had succeeded in cutting their way up through the scuttle with axes, and were arming themselves with cutlasses and pistols taken from the deck-house in which the carpenter slept. The carpenter, who was a very powerfully-built Frenchman, put himself at their head and bravely called upon them to follow him and rescue the captain and officers, little knowing that Merrill himself was leading the pirates.

Surrender !' cried Merrill, levelling

"Up, up, all of you !" shouted Merrill fiercely to his followers ; and leaving the unfortunate captain, mate and steward to breathe their last in the ensanguined cabin, he sprang up the companion. They were only just in time, for at the break of the poop they met the rescuing seamen, headed by the carpenter.

"Surrender !" cried Merrill, levelling his pistol at the Frenchman, "the captain and mate are dead and the ship is ours." A bullet from the gallant carpenter's pistol was the reply he received ; and then began a savage struggle for the possession of the deck, Merrill and his men fighting as only desperate men with halters round their necks fight. But they were out-numbered by three to one, and must certainly have been overpowered in a few minutes, when Worcester gave a shout of joy.

"Here's Captain Rowley's boat coming alongside ;" and making a spring he actually

jumped off the poop on top of the Frenchman and bore him down upon the main-
deck, hoping, as he told Kingston, that
he might be able to save the poor fellow's
life, and end all further and useless
slaughter. But the loyal part of the crew,
not knowing, of course, that Rowley with
half a dozen men actually was alongside,
continued the struggle, the carpenter
having succeeded in throwing off Worcester
and then felling him by a blow on the
head with the butt of his pistol.

Followed by his smugglers, Rowley
clambered over the side and rushed to
Merrill's assistance, and it was then, said
Worcester, that one of Merrill's men slashed
off the hand of the man Miranda as he was
trying to clamber up on the poop. In a
few minutes the carpenter was cut down by
the stroke of a cutlass, and then the surviv-
ing members of the crew who had so gallantly
stuck to the poor Frenchman threw down
their arms and surrendered, though not until

Rowley himself had received a slight bullet wound in the arm and a blow on the head from the back of an axe, which stunned him.

Merrill at once took command, and ordered the men who had surrendered into Rowley's boat. Two oars only were given them, with some water and provisions, and they were told to make for the land, then twenty miles distant. Then the bodies of the dead men, among whom was the carpenter, were thrown overboard, all sail made, and the brig stood in along the land for Arica, where Vigors boarded her with the new second officer.

Horrified at the negro's story, Kingston was at first at a loss for words to express himself. Then he earnestly besought Worcester to be true to his word, and help him to recapture the ship, and carry her back to her rightful owners.

"I will, sah. As true as God is above, I will," he said solemnly, holding his hand up to heaven.

CHAPTER VI.

BURNING with indignation at the manner in which he had been deceived and trapped, Kingston eagerly discussed the proposed seizure of the brig with his new ally, and the more they talked of the matter, the more hopeful he became of eventually turning the tables on Rowley and Merrill, and carrying the vessel to Valparaiso. For it maddened him to think that not only Captain Forestier, but Rosa as well, would naturally imagine that he had, out of pure revenge for his abrupt dismissal from Forestier's service, joined Rowley and his gang when they seized the brig. Forestier could not fail to hear of his having met the

notorious *contrabandista* Rowley at Arica,
and of his being on friendly terms with him
just prior to the capture of the *Jalasco* and
the murder of the captain, mate, and some
of the crew ; for even had those of the crew
whose lives had been spared, met with
disaster (which was however, unlikely) and
not reached the shore, there were plenty of
people in Arica who could, and no doubt
would, acquaint the Forestiers of his seem-
ing intimacy with both Rowley and Vigors.
What else could Rosa think, he asked
himself again and again, but that he had
deliberately taken part in piracy and
murder ?

For nearly half an hour he and Worcester
conversed on the matter, and then, fearing
their absence might cause comment, they
separated, each returning to the boat by
a different route. They had agreed upon
the absolute necessity of caution in their
demeanour to each other when on board the
brig, for it would never do to let Rowley

or Merrill know that Kingston had the slightest knowledge of the dark deed done that night off Arica.

With such an object in view as the re-capture of the *Jalasco*, it was not a difficult task for him to dissimulate, and so when the boat returned he was more cheerful than usual, 'chaffed' the captain on his narrow escape of a few hours previously, and even indulged in some apparently good-natured jests at the expense of the two cowardly seamen who had failed to come to their assistance when they were struggling for their lives in the water.

Although the brig still required pumping twice in every watch, the weather was now very fine, and for days and days she con-tinued her course without lifting tack or sheet, for she was now in the very heart of the steady south-east trades, and after leav-ing the Paumotu group, spun steadily along over a smooth sea, till the lonely but beautiful Suwarrow's Lagoon was sighted.

Here Kingston tried to induce Rowley to
enter the lagoon, and endeavour to get at
the leak or leaks, for the place was unin-
habited, and afforded good natural facilities
for beaching the vessel. He had twice
visited the atoll years before, and on one
occasion the ship to which he belonged had
remained there for two or three weeks,
wooding, watering and refreshing the crew.

But Rowley would not be tempted; he
was too anxious to push on, and unless the
ship made more water he would not, he
said, bother about the leak, and put up
with a delay that might mean their losing
the south-east trades. There certainly was
some force in his contention, so Kingston
again let the matter drop.

He and Worcester were careful not to be
seen talking to each other except on matters
concerning the ship, but nevertheless they
did sometimes contrive to whisper a few
hurried words to each other, and on of these
occasions the negro told Kingston that he

believed the young Peruvian steward, José Pimental, could be gained over, as he had told him (Worcester) that his mind was much disturbed at the part he had taken in the seizure of the brig and the murder of the captain, mate, steward, and carpenter.

"He been told me, sah," whispered the boatswain, "dat he can't sleep at night fo' thinking dat he boun' to go to hell if any of de bullets he fired dat night when Rowley came on board, hit and killed one ob dose sailor men. He says dat all de money he will get will go in masses for dere souls an' his own, an' I'se been encouragin' him to think dat he did kill one ob 'em, sure 'nuff."

"That is good news, bo'sun, and we must try and sound him some time. I too, have noticed that at times he seems very despondent, and scarcely speaks all day."

The south-east trades carried the *Jalasco* to within a hundred miles of the north of Samoa, and then followed a long spell of heavy westerly weather, and Rowley, ever impatient, in trying to thrash the brig to windward, succeeded in so straining her, that the pumps had to be attended to more frequently than ever. Several sails were lost, and the crew began to show signs of discontent. Kingston suggested the advisability of putting in to Samoa, where the natives were friendly, and where the ship could be repaired, but Rowley, though he himself was now anxious about the brig's condition, made first one and then another excuse, and both Kingston and Worcester now felt certain that he would not put into any port in the South Seas where there was a probability of meeting other European vessels.

And they were right in their conclusions —the man was afraid of running up against the American frigate *Vincennes* or one of her consorts, then in the South Pacific on an exploring cruise; both he and Merrill had heard in Callao that the

commodore intended to make a detailed
survey of the Samoan group, and would
probably remain there some months. So,
much to the disappointment of the second
officer and his ally, Rowley continued to
fight stubbornly against the head wind,
but announced his willingness to put into
any one of the Ellice Island lagoons which
Kingston might suggest, and there repair
the ship.

"We must be patient," said Kingston
to the negro one day when the two were
in the hold together overhauling some
stores; "but had we put into Samoa we
should have been sure to have met with
at least a whaleship or two, or a trading
vessel. And then the thing would be easy
enough—with the help of half a dozen
armed men we could capture the whole
bag of the infernal villains." Then he
went on to say that he had in readiness
a letter, detailing the whole story of the
Jalasco, which he intended to send on

board to the captain of the first ship they
met, providing he could get the opportunity.

At last the wind hauled round to the
south-east again, and kept there, and
although the crew were almost constantly
at the pumps, their discontent vanished
somewhat with the fine weather, for the
vessel was put under every stitch of
canvas she could set, and Rowley had told
them that in a few days he would put
into a lagoon known to the second mate,
where, after the ship had been repaired,
they should have a week's liberty on
shore.

This lagoon, of which the captain had
spoken, was one of the Ellice group of
atolls, called " De Peyster's Island " on
the poor chart on board the *Jalasco*, but
known to Kingston and other men who
had sailed among the South Pacific islands
by its native name of Nukufetau. He
had once before visited it, and knew enough

of the inhabitants to justify him in telling Rowley that they would render such assistance as he might ask for.

The *Jalasco* was spinning along one night at ten knots over a gently heaving sea, when Kingston, after telling the mate that Puka Puka (Danger Island) ought to be sighted soon after daylight, went below. Merrill, he knew, would see that a good look-out was kept, so there would be no danger of running ashore on some unknown reef or island. For an hour or so he did not turn in, employing himself in preparing some lines which he intended to use in the morning for bonito fishing.

From the opposite side of the cabin he could hear Rowley's deep, heavy breathing, and overhead the light but steady footfall of the mate as he paced to and fro on his watch. At the foot of the companion lay the young Peruvian steward Pimental, wrapped up in his coarse Chilian poncho. This man slept in a berth off the pantry, but he never turned in until after ten o'clock, for at that time it was always the practice to serve the officer of the watch— and anyone else aft who desired it—with coffee, and Kingston, though it was a novel custom to him, thought it a very good one, and on this particular night decided not to turn in till after José had brought the coffee and the French biscuits served with it.

As he finished seizing on the last hook to the three lines he had prepared, he stepped out into the main cabin, and glanced at the clock to see the time. The steward heard his step, roused himself and went on deck to the galley, and just then Merrill entered the cabin and went to his room. He reappeared in a moment with a piece of wire in his hand, stood under the swinging lamp, and began to prod the stem of his pipe (which he always smoked at night instead of cigars), which was evidently stopped. Kingston could not

8

help thinking to himself that **Mr. Merrill's** ideas of discipline were pretty elastic, when he could thus coolly come below during his watch on deck to clean his pipe.

"Well, she's ripping gaily along to-night," he said, holding the unscrewed stem of his pipe up to the light so as to see if it was clear.

"Yes," replied the second officer, "we ought to see Danger Island at daylight, and then we can keep her W. by N. for De Peyster's Lagoon."

"What's the distance?" asked Merrill, who seemed inclined to be talkative, for he sat down and leisurely began cutting a pipeful of tobacco.

"Just two hundred miles; if this breeze holds good, we ought to be inside the lagoon in eighteen or twenty hours after we pass Danger Island."

"Well, I reckon I'll be glad enough to see those pumps quiet again. We've had enough——"

· "*Man overboard!*"

The cry rang out so shrill, sharp, and weirdly, that Kingston caught his breath. But for an instant only, for ere it was repeated, he and Merrill together sprang on deck, and the latter ran to the wheel. As he brought the brig to the wind, he gave his orders in loud, clear tones, and so quickly were they executed that in less than five minutes the starboard quarter boat was in the water with Kingston and four hands in her.

"He can't be far astern," cried Merrill, as the boat veered astern, and a blue light was lit by one of the hands and held over the rail ; "keep hailing, Mr. Kingston, and I'll run a light up to the gaff."

"Aye, aye," replied Kingston, who, as his crew bent to their oars, heard the captain's voice ordering away a second boat.

The night was fairly clear, starlit, and the sea smooth, so there was every chance of the man being saved, especially con-

sidering the expeditious manner in which
the boat was lowered, and if he was at all
able to swim. Heading the boat for the
spot where the man would probably be
found, and hailing every minute, he scanned
the starlit surface of the ocean everywhere
around. Then for the first time he asked
his crew who it was, and, to his intense
sorrow, was told that it was the boatswain.

"The last I saw of him," said one of the
men in a low voice, "was when he was
standing on the topgallant foc'sc'le. He
must have tripped over one of the sheets
and fallen overboard."

"Stop pulling," said the officer, "and let
us hail together."

No response came to their united call, and
again they bent to their oars, listening
carefully.

Rowley's boat had now left the brig,
which continued to burn blue lights; she
stood out so clearly that had the un-

fortunate man been alive, and anywhere within two miles, he could not have failed to have seen her. Every now and then both boats would cease pulling, hail together, and listen, but no answering cry came back.

For a full hour the boats continued their search, and then Rowley hailed Kingston.

"I fear the poor fellow has gone," he said.

"I fear so too; but yet he is a great swimmer, and may perhaps be half-stunned, and unable to call out. For God's sake, don't give up all hope of finding him for another hour."

"No, indeed, I won't, not for two hours or more," answered the captain, with such undoubted sincerity in his tones that a dark and growing suspicion of foul play that had taken possession of Kingston, died away as far as Rowley was concerned.

And for two hours more, both brig and boats kept up the search, till Kingston himself knew that all hope was gone—the poor negro, he knew, had been called before his Maker. Silently he turned the boat's head, and the crew pulled up to Rowley, and together they returned to the brig. Then the boats were hoisted up, and the vessel put upon her course again.

By this time it was Kingston's watch on deck, but before relieving the mate he went below to change his thin clothes for warmer garments, as the night air was beginning to feel chilly. Rowley was seated at the cabin table, his chin in his hands, and looking worried and depressed. He nodded to Kingston without speaking, and pointed to a decanter of brandy and glasses. His own glass was before him, as yet untouched.

"Mr. Kingston," he said at last, in a curious, shaky voice, "I would give a thousand pounds to see that man here before me. Once, in a moment of passion, I drew a pistol on him, but God knows I was sorry enough for it afterwards, and——"

Suddenly, from somewhere in the main cabin, there came the sound· of a heavy, anguished sob.

"Who. is that?" cried Rowley, starting to his feet.

A low, half-suppressed cry, as if of some-one in mortal terror, answered him, and then José, the steward, appeared at the door of his cabin. His figure was trembling from head to foot, and his eyes had the look of those of one who had suddenly awakened in the midst of some terrible dream.

"What is the matter with you?" demanded Rowley. "Have you seen a ghost?"

His question recalled the man to his senses. He came forward to the table, and although Kingston could see that he was terribly agitated, he spoke sensibly and clearly enough.

"Si, senor captain," he answered in Spanish, "I have seen ghosts in my dreams for many nights past, and now——"

"Go back to your bunk, you drivelling lunatic," cried Rowley with sudden fury, and he advanced threateningly toward the Peruvian.

"You may kill me if you like, senor," replied the man unwaveringly, "a man can die but once;" he paused a moment, "and I would rather die now and be judged for my sins than suffer as I do day and night." He ceased, then looking fixedly, first at Rowley, and then at Kingston, he said quietly to the latter—

"Senor, the poor negro was murdered. I did not see it done, but I have proof."

"Ha," and Kingston turned quickly and sternly to the captain, whose florid face blanched, "ha, I thought as much. Speak out, man. Tell me what you know. What did you see?"

"Aye, tell us," said Rowley, steadying his voice, as he went and closed the cabin door, and then returned to the head of the table, "tell us all you know, for I call God to witness that if what you say is true, I am guiltless of any part in it," and as he spoke his eyes met those of Kingston · without flinching.

"Let the man speak," said Kingston sternly.

"Senor, I will tell you all, but first look at this."

He stepped swiftly to his pantry, and brought back a hat, which he placed on the table. It was of a dark grey felt with a wide brim, and both Rowley and Kingston at once recognised it as the boatswain's, and they both started when they saw that it was splashed with blood.

"Look," he said in low, distinct tones, "I picked that up under the break of the foc's'cle; it was lying on the waterways, where it had fallen."

"Go on," said Kingston, with blazing eyes; "when was this?"

"After the boats had left, senor; I brought it to the cabin. I would have

thrown it overboard, but now I thank the
Holy Virgin that I had not the courage to
do so, for then I should be helping to conceal murder."

Then in a few further words he told the
rest of his story. When he went to the
galley, he had seen the boatswain standing
on the topgallant forecastle, smoking. Two
of the crew were also there—one of them,
Antonio, was on the look-out, the other, who
was a man named Texeira, and not in the
mate's watch, was sitting down on the starboard side singing; the rest of the watch
below were under the topgallant forecastle
playing cards. After he had made coffee,
he put it aside for a few minutes to settle,
and happening to look out of the galley door,
was somewhat surprised to see that the men
who were playing cards had put out their
light, and that there was an unusual silence.
Quite ten minutes passed before he took up
the coffee to carry it aft, during which time
he heard nothing but the noise of the brig

as she cut through the water, and he was half-way along the deck when he heard the cry of " man overboard."

The captain and Kingston heard him in silence. Then the latter rose, and pointed to the blood-stained hat.

"Captain Rowley, there was no need for us to lower a boat; the poor man has been foully murdered. Call the men aft, and question them, or by heaven, I will go for'ard and myself shoot the man whom I firmly believe is the murderer—that sneaking cut-throat Antonio."

" For God's sake, do nothing hastily," said Rowley in a husky voice. " I am with you in this. I swear to you that neither I nor Merrill——"

" Ha!" and Kingston struck his clenched hand fiercely on the table, and bent his deep set eyes on the captain, "now I begin to doubt you both ! What brought Mr. Merrill down here, talking to me when it was his watch on deck ? By the God above us, I believe you both to have been party to this cowardly murder? *I know who and what you are.* I know how I have been deceived and ensnared by your lying tongue into sailing with pirates and murderers!"

The fatal words were no sooner spoken than he inwardly cursed his folly, for now he had shown his hand, and his life perhaps would be the penalty. He sprang to his cabin, seized his pistols, which he had always kept loaded, and then stepped out and faced Rowley.

"Put down your pistols, man," said the captain, who spoke calmly and quietly, "your life is in no danger from me. Some-one has betrayed us, I can see. But I never meant any harm to you. I had to lie pretty hard to you in Arica, I admit. Desperate men have to do desperate things. I suppose you know that this brig is not the *Blossom*?"

"I know the whole story."

"Then the less said about it the better.

"He sprang to his cabin and seized his pistols."

[*See page* 124.

I mean to stick to my bargain with you——"

"And I refuse to do duty with pirates and murderers. "

"Steady, steady. Let us talk. And put away those pistols. I swear to you that though I have deceived you in the past, I will not do so again; but the crew would murder you in five minutes if they thought it was necessary for their safety. That they have murdered that poor nigger I don't doubt; but whether you believe me or not, I call God to witness that neither I nor the mate had anything to do with it directly or indirectly. " He stopped, and then addressed the Peruvian.

"Go on deck, you, and tell Mr. Merrill to come down here quietly. Sit down, please, Mr. Kingston. I am not the cold-blooded scoundrel you judge me to be. "

In spite of himself, Kingston believed the man, and already he had decided on the course that was best for him to follow. He put his pistols back into his bunk, and then quietly seated himself opposite the captain. Merrill entered.

"Tom," said Rowley, "the game is up as far as Mr. Kingston is concerned. He knows the whole story."

The American took the news very coolly.

"Thought it would come out somehow."

"How he got to know it does not matter. He does know it, and that's the long and short of it. But he thinks that as you and I are responsible for the deaths of the captain, mate, and other men who were on board this ship, that we also are concerned in the death of the bo'sun." Then he repeated the Peruvian steward's story to the mate, who listened without making any interruption, even when Rowley told him Kingston's suspicions of himself for coming down below when it was his watch on deck.

A deep flush tinged the American's impassive face for a moment or two as he raised his eyes to Kingston, and in a few but passionate words he disclaimed absolutely any knowledge of the negro's murder.

"I came down below, because my pipe was stopped up," he added, "and if the man was knocked on the head and thrown overboard—as there seems to be no doubt of—it was done while I was here in the cabin. I would have defended his life with my own before I would have been a party to his murder in cold blood."

There was a brief silence, and then Rowley looked first at Merrill and then at Kingston. Then he said with foolish haste, "Will you come in with us, Kingston? We will deal fair and square with you. Will you take ten thousand dollars?"

"I will take none of your blood-stained money. I have always been an honest man and will die one. And I tell you frankly that while I will stand by the agreement you induced me to sign to navi-

gate the brig to Macao, and will do duty
as second mate, I will promise no more.
You understand what I mean."

"I do," said Rowley, who, unscrupulous
and hardened as he was, could yet admire
courage. And then he was in hopes that
in time he could induce Kingston to change
his mind.

At daylight next morning, Danger Island
was in sight, and Kingston came to the
captain.

"The steward tells me that he fears—
and he has reason to fear—he will be
murdered by those cut-throats for'ard if he
remains on board, and has begged me to
ask you to let him go ashore at this island.
The people there will treat him well, and
he can leave there by the first whaleship
that calls. For heaven's sake let him go.
We have had enough bloodshed already."

Rowley did not hesitate. The brig was
hove-to, a boat was lowered, and José
Pimental, with his chest, and a present of

a hundred dollars from Kingston—he steadfastly refused to take any money from
Rowley — stepped into the boat and was
pulled ashore.

Before the Peruvian left the brig Kingston shook hands with him in the cabin,
and contrived to tell him that he hoped to
recapture· the *Jalasco* ere long, and if so,
he would come back to Danger Island and
pick him up. And José, taking the officer's
hand in his own, kissed it in silent gratitude.

CHAPTER VII.

BACK to the deep, placid bosom of Nukufetau Lagoon.

Soon after sunrise on the morning following the arrival of the *Jalasco*, and whilst
only the usual armed anchor watch of two
men — one aft and one for'ard — were on
deck, a swarm of canoes put off from the
village and surrounded the ship.

The captain and officers at once made
their appearance, and Fonu, who com-
manded the flotilla, came on board, and
informed Rowley that Potiri the head priest,
having consulted the oracles of the gods
concerning the treatment of the ship's com-

pany, and having received a favourable reply commanding the people to render them assistance, he, Fonu, with a hundred 'strong' men, now awaited his instructions. . Rowley at once gave orders to get the guns rafted ashore. This work, which was supervised by the second officer, was soon accomplished, a number of canoes, lashed together and loosely decked with flat pieces of light but strong timber, making an excellent raft, capable of sustaining the weight of the brig's armament of ten guns.

Kingston, whose mind was as actively employed as he was physically, was especially energetic and cheerful, and encouraged the natives by voice and gesture in their operations. He was particularly anxious to get into conversation with Fonu, which he soon accomplished, and the young chief was delighted when, after the guns had been safely landed on the shore of the little island abreast of the *Jalasco*, Kingston told him that he had previously visited

Nukufetau, and named the ship (the *Nina Casalle*), which Fonu remembered.

Rowley, and Merrill as well, could not but feel pleased that day at the change in the demeanour of the second mate. Twice during the forenoon he had accepted Rowley's invitation to drink with him in the cabin, and even Merrill, who was an unusually astute personage, was deceived, and began to believe that after all, Kingston was 'coming round' and might eventually yield to the tempting bribe offered him, and cast in his lot with theirs.

Kingston had made up his mind to play a desperate game. Rowley had deceived him cruelly, and now he resolved to cast aside all his former scruples and resort to dissimulation to gain his ends, which were simply all that he held dear in life—the re-establishment of his own reputation with Captain Forestier by the recapture of the brig and the regaining of the affection of the woman he loved; for how could he, he thought, expect her to now regard him with aught but aversion ?

During his many years' wanderings among the islands of the South and North Pacific, he had acquired a fair knowledge of many of the Polynesian dialects, for nearly every whaleship and trading vessel carried then, as they do at this present time, a number of natives among their crews. This knowledge he now proceeded to put to use by conversing with the islanders who were working at lightening the brig, and in particular he devoted his attention to Fonu, paying him many compliments upon his great stature and strength, and insinuating that he (Kingston) very much desired him to be his *soa* or friend. Fonu was of course highly flattered, and very quickly responded to the advances made by the white man.

The work of lightening the ship went on so expeditiously, that on the third day she was floated up over the flat patch of rock, and as soon as the tide fell, an examination was made of her bottom. The damage she had sustained proved to be much more serious than was imagined—half a dozen of her planks on the starboard side between keel and bilge were so badly injured that it would be absolutely necessary to replace them by new ones, which would have to be sawn from out of some of the spare spars carried on deck. Kingston was secretly pleased, for although he was apparently working very hard in assisting Rowley and Merrill to get the ship ready for sea again, he really wanted to delay her until he had completed the plans he had in view.

Before four days had passed, he had made the acquaintance of the old head priest Potiri, whose ruling passion was avarice, to which Kingston duly, but secretly, ministered by presenting him with several pounds of powder and a few hundred musket balls, which he surreptitiously abstracted from the magazine and sent ashore one night by one of Potiri's sons.

This present he supplemented on another occasion by a couple of bottles of fiery 'Pisco,' for which the priest had an intense liking, and there was soon established between the two a tacit, but unspoken understanding, the white man throwing out mysterious hints that he would confer great future benefits on him if he, Potiri, would meet certain wishes of his which would be made known to him at some other time.

Before a week had passed, Rowley and Merrill noticed that the second mate, usually a very abstemious man, now changed his habits and never refused to join when asked to drink with them in the cabin, and occasionally ordered the steward to bring him liquor to his berth. Then, too, they could not but observe that he was becoming somewhat rough and rude in his manner and language, and frequently commented to them on the good looks of some of the native girls, who now visited the ship, and remained idling about the decks all day. For he was now playing his part determinedly.

There was one remarkably handsome girl in particular, whose name was Vailavea, to whom he paid the most ostentatious attention, making her a present of a necklace of silver beads, and a gaily coloured rebozo, which he had bought in Arica months before. The young lady was, of course, intensely pleased with these marks of his favour, and assumed a haughtiness of demeanour to her girlish companions that would have been amusing to the donor, did he not realise that poor Vailavea took things seriously, and soon began to openly show the tender feelings with which she regarded him. But the dangerous game he was playing had to be played perfectly, and although he hated to be obliged to practise such duplicity upon the simple-minded girl, he let her imagine that the tenderness was mutual, and endured her artless display of affection as well as he could.

He could see that, like all Polynesian women, she would soon become passionately jealous of him; but he consoled himself with the reflection and belief that, on the other hand, she would come to no harm through him, and would be equally as quick to reconcile herself to his loss when he told her that his duty called him to his own country—and she was handsomely compensated. And the latter he intended to do.

In the lower hold of the brig, when she was seized by Rowley, were two thousand hides, which represented at least four or five thousand dollars. The lower layers of these had become so soaked with salt water, owing to the brig leaking after running ashore, that the captain, when the vessel was being lightened, had intended either throwing them overboard, or giving them to the natives; but Kingston, who now seemed very solicitous about everything connected with the brig, urged him not to throw away such valuable property when the hides could easily be carried ashore, dried, and re-stowed.

"They are worth four or five thousand dollars in New York or Boston," he said casually, "and ought to be worth as much or more to us in any China port, so it would be folly to throw them away."

Rowley was quick to note the 'us' in what was apparently a careless remark, and later on mentioned it to Merrill.

"Reckon it's that girl Vailavea who is bringing him to his senses," said the American, cynically; "she's handsome enough for anything. If he keeps on liquoring up as he is doing now, he'll forget all about the girl in Valparaiso and take to the red-skin. Wouldn't mind betting you a ten-dollar piece, Ben, that before we bend sails again, he'll tell you he's going to stick to his new flame, and want to take her away with him."

"All the better for us if he would," said

Rowley with a laugh ; "nothing would please me more. We must get him to come in us somehow, and this girl has ' happened along' just at the right time. She's as pretty as a picture, so I don't wonder much at his being so taken up with her. As for me," he added reflectively, "I never had the time nor inclination to fool about women. It's wonderful what a pretty woman can do, though."

"It is," said Merrill, chewing his cigar ; "they can do a power of mischief."

The little island on which the hides were being dried was called Teafuana, and the beach on which they lay was in full view from the deck of the *Jalasco*. Further back from the beach, and situated among a grove of breadfruit trees, were two or three houses, only the roofs of which were visible from the brig. Kingston had working for him about a dozen natives, men and women, and it was his practice to start off immediately after breakfast, and superintend the cleaning, drying, and refolding of the hides. A narrow path which traversed the centre of the islet from end to end communicated with the village on the main island, except, of course, where a narrow strip of fordable water divided the two. Encompassed as it was on both sides by countless coco-palms growing very thickly together, this path could not be discerned from any point seaward, and except Kingston, no one on board the brig knew of its existence. Yet for some time he had used it frequently, at least once a day, to visit the old priest Potiri; and Potiri, in his turn, had on several occasions come to the little islet, and conversed with him in one of the houses in the breadfruit grove.

By this time Kingston had to a certain extent taken both Fonu and the girl Vailavea into his confidence. The latter, when her lover—if we may so call him— was either visiting or being visited by Potiri, always remained on the beach with the rest of the islanders who were employed with the hides, and when either Rowley or Merrill did come ashore, which was infrequent, to see how Kingston was getting on, the girl, as soon as she saw the boat put off from the ship, at once slipped away and gave the alarm, so that the second officer always had time to meet them when they landed.

It had now become an open secret with the natives that the *sui alii elua* (the second mate) was an especial favourite of the head priest, and that he was to be treated with every respect and consideration. And Potiri himself had judiciously put it abroad that the captain had not, and would not, treat them as generously as he should do for their services, but that he, Potiri, was guarding their interests, and would instruct them how to act later on—after he had 'consulted the gods,' as usual.

One bright, cool morning, Rowley, at the breakfast table, told Merrill and Kingston that he had heard there were a great number of pigeons on an island on the weather side of the lagoon called Sakuru, and that he intended going there with a boat's crew after breakfast, and have a day's sport.

"I would not take too many of the men away with you, if I were you," said Kingston.

"Why, you don't think the natives would be up to any mischief, do you?" asked Rowley in sudden alarm.

"No, I have no reason to think that," replied Kingston, suavely; "but at the same time it's wrong putting a blind trust in them because they are so friendly with us. There is no knowing what might happen if you were away with half of the hands, and two or three hundred of them came on board, and perhaps tried to steal—a row might start at any moment, and they are a very easily excited lot. The *Romany Lass*, sandalwooder, was cut-off in this very group, just through sheer carelessness—the captain gave the natives a keg of rum and the result was that they became maddened with drink, killed him and all his crew, and plundered and burnt the ship. So we might as well be careful."

Rowley was again secretly delighted at Kingston's interest in their common safety, and made some jocular remark that he thought Kingston's sweetheart was pretty sure to warn him if her countrymen meant any mischief.

After breakfast he started off, with only two hands and a native guide, for Sakuru, leaving Merrill in charge of the brig, and Kingston to attend to the hides as usual.

This was just what the latter wanted, for that morning he was to meet Potiri, Fonu, and the head chief in secret conference, and openly lay his plans before them. And he now felt sure that neither Rowley nor Merrill had any suspicions about him.

CHAPTER VIII

As soon as Kingston landed, he sent his boat back to the ship, and walked quietly up through the natives who were working at the hides, to the house where he knew Potiri and the others were awaiting him. There was no fear of his being disturbed by anyone from the brig, for Merrill had some of the hands employed in making ready the lower hold floor for the hides, and others in caulking the decks. The *Jalasco* had been thoroughly and effectively repaired, and was to be floated on the following evening at high water, and the guns and heavy stores rafted off early on the succeeding day.

The beautiful Vailavea met him with a

144

smiling face at the door of the house. In her hand she carried a coco-nut shell filled with fresh, sweet toddy, which she always brought to him every time he came ashore.

" 'Tis not so cool as it should be," she said timidly as she watched him raise the shell to his lips and drink, "but the night was very hot and close, for there was no wind."

" 'Tis cool enough, Vailavea. And, if it were not, dost think I should grumble?"

She turned her dark eyes up to his and smiled again, and he felt a flush mantle his cheek when he thought of the cruel part he was compelled to play in making the innocent young girl believe that she had gained his heart. He touched her cheek gently with his hand and passed into the house.

The dwelling, though it contained but one room, was large, and displayed in the interior great skill and care in its construction and furnishing. The floor—if it could be so called—was formed of a thick layer of small, round, and snow-white coral pebbles worn

10

perfectly smooth by attrition on the beach.
In the centre it was uncovered, but all
round the sides of the apartment were
layers of soft and highly ornamented mats.
As the house was under the care of Potiri
and his fellow-priests it could not be used
or even entered by women, and consequently
there was an entire absence of any articles
devoted to domestic purposes, such as
cooking utensils, sleeping mats, etc. In
place of these were numbers of elaborately
carved clubs, hideous wooden masks, and
huge double-edged wooden swords, ten to
fifteen feet long and edged with large
sharks' teeth. These weapons, though not
then used in warfare as frequently as in
times gone by, were highly treasured, each
one possessing some particular *mana* or
sanctity, and all being especially devoted to
the god Erikobai. All round the beauti-
fully-thatched wall were numbers of skulls,
all highly polished and set side by side on
a shelf which ran round the entire room.

These grim objects were the treasured relics
of noted men, and were treated with the
utmost respect and reverence.

On the matted floor of the house were
seated five natives—old Potiri, clothed in
his wild and fanciful costume of head priest,
two other priests, Fonu, and the head chief.
Kingston greeted them all in turn, and then
sat down to join in a preliminary smoke.
No sound from without disturbed the silence,
except now and then the faint murmur of
voices from the beach beyond the grove of
broad-leaved trees which surrounded the
house, and, further away to the westward,
the ever-restless beat of the surf upon the
outer reef.

At a sign from old Potiri, one of the
younger priests rose, stepped outside, and
putting a small conch shell to his lips blew
a faint note, hardly louder than the cry of a
sea-bird. Then came footsteps, as thirty or
forty stalwart natives filed into the house
one by one, and sat down in silence.

"Now," said old Potiri, first bending his keen black eyes upon the assemblage and then turning to Fonu, "let the white man tell us all that which he hath told thee and me."

"Nay," said Kingston, in the native dialect, "I am well content to let Fonu speak, for he knoweth my story, and I have but scant knowledge of the tongue of this land to tell so long a tale."

So Fonu, to whom Kingston had told the true story of the *Jalasco* in detail, from the time he met Rowley at Arica to the day she entered the lagoon, retold it to the assembled people, who listened with the most intense interest.

"All this is true," said Potiri, when Fonu had ceased. "I knew it even before the white man told of it" (Kingston stroked his face to conceal a smile). "I knew it when the big, red-faced captain first came and lied to us, for the gods had spoken to me. Now this man who hath just spoken is a good man, and hath come to me for help, and help he shall have. It is his desire to take back this ship which hath been stolen, and restore it to the rightful owner. And because of the help that we shall give him to seize and bind the captain and those with him, he will reward us well, for he is a man of a very generous and great heart— so great that it filleth his body from his loins upward. Let him now tell us of the things that shall be ours when once we have bound these men on the ship."

Kingston had already promised the cunning old rascal some especial gifts for himself, and he (Potiri) had given him strict instructions not to make any mention of these when describing the presents he intended to make to the people generally.

So once more Fonu interpreted for Kingston and said—"These are the things, O Potiri, Voice of the god Erikobai and the lesser gods, that the white man will give to us : Ten muskets, new and unsoiled, two kegs of bullets and two bags of bullets, and many caps; two large and two small kegs of powder; ten swords such as the sailors carry at their waists; ten pistols, each with much powder, bullets and caps; a cask of grog which shall be half a *gafa* (half a fathom) high, thick in the belly and strong to the taste and smell (this evoked a murmur of applause); two thousand sticks of good tobacco, which is in a great round box like unto a cask; twenty short Spanish axes; a hundred fathoms of blue cloth (navy blue calico); two casks in each of which are more than five hundred ship biscuits."

A murmured *s-s-s-s* of delight broke from the listening men, but Fonu was not yet finished.

"And of the eight great looking-glasses (mirror panels) which are set in the cabin, two shall be cut out from the wood in which they are set, and one shall be for Potiri to set in the temple of Erikobai, and the other for our chief, so that all the people may look into it at any time."

These mirrors, with which the main cabin of the *Jalasco* was ornamented, were the wonder and delight of the natives, none of whom, except perhaps Fonu, had seen anything so magnificent, and so when Fonu had suggested to Kingston that he should present one or two of them to the people, the latter at once acquiesced: As a matter of fact, he was prepared, if necessary, to give away all the internal decorations of the brig if the greedy old Potiri wanted them. As it was, the total value of all the articles he was giving away would be under three hundred pounds in English money—and what was three hundred, or five hundred, or even a thousand pounds, when compared with the value of the brig herself and her cargo, quite apart from the specie she carried?

However, the announcement of the intended presentation of the two 'looking-glasses'—each over six feet in length and eighteen inches in width—whereby they would be able to regard their all but naked and stalwart figures at full length, brought the natives to such a pitch of excitement, that for some minutes Fonu was unable to make himself heard. But silence established again, he resumed—

"All these things shall be given to us by this our friend, for whom I speak. They shall be put out upon the deck of the ship on the day that we, the men of Nukufetau, make prisoners the captain and the second captain (the mate) and the sailor men. And beyond and above these things he will yet let us keep all that which was promised to us by the captain for the work which we have done. This white man is a just man, and will deny us nothing of the price of our labour. That is all."

Kingston looked anxiously at him, fearing that he had forgotten a very important matter, but Fonu only smiled and began again.

"That is all of that matter, but there is yet more to be spoken of. When this our friend hath made himself master of the ship, he will yet be but one man. And how can one man sail the ship back to the country from which she was stolen? Now, these are his words—'Let six, or if not six, five, or even four men come with and help me to work the ship. To each man I shall give a great reward, and pledge my word that he shall come safely back to Nukufetau, though not for many months. If I bring them not back myself, then shall they return in one of the many *vaka ia manu* (whale ships) which, before they sail to these islands, come to Valparaiso. The man in America to whom the ship belongeth is a just and a generous man.'"

In an instant ten or a dozen young men eagerly volunteered. Three of them had been to sea before, and Kingston saw that he would have no difficulty in obtaining a full crew to work the brig to Valparaiso. Fonu had, the day before, expressed his

wish to come with him, and his example
alone was sufficient to make the others eager,
especially as the wily old Potiri vouched for
their safe return, and the protection of the
gods during their absence.

"It is well," said Kingston, who had
come prepared with pen, ink and paper;
" now shall I write down here on this paper.
the names of those men who sail with me.
For, as I have told Fonu, it may be that
ere many months have passed, there will
come here two or three fighting ships
(men-of-war) belonging to America.[1]   They
do but come here to see these islands, and
learn how ye of Nukufetau live, and ye may
show this paper to the chief of the fighting
ships, and tell him all these things which
have happened. And so that my *tuhi*
(writing) shall confirm to him all that thou
tellest, I shall, when the ship is recovered
again, give thee a letter for him in which is
written down the evil deeds of these men

[1] Captain Wilkes' (U.S.) Exploring Expedition.

who have murdered and robbed, and how I besought thy help. This will please the chief of the fighting ships, and he will commend thee abroad as true men, and many ships will come to this land for food and water—ships that before would have feared to anchor here lest the people should have proved treacherous, and killed them as hath been done many times in these islands."

This was a particularly pleasing announcement to his audience; for although the people of Nukufetau had once cut off a whaleship or two in their haste, they had repented at their leisure, for the bad reputation they had acquired had prevented many vessels from touching at the island, and they were now eager to show their friendliness and goodwill towards white people.

The letter to "the chief of the fighting ships" to which he had alluded, he had already written, and was at that moment sewn up in the breast lining of his coat. It was addressed "To the Commodore of the

United States Exploring Expedition," which
was certain to visit the Ellice group, and
set forth in detail the particulars of the
piracy of the *Jalasco*, and the action he was
taking in recapturing her. Then, too, he
thought, luck might go against him; the
Jalasco might be fated never to reach
Valparaiso, and it would be well for him, if
he were destined to perish, to leave some
written record that would, perhaps long
after, clear his memory to Captain Forestier
and his daughter.

Then the principal matter of all was
entered upon—the actual planning of how
Rowley, Merrill and the crew were to be
seized, Kingston earnestly impressing upon
his native associates his desire that no blood
should be shed. As regarded the disposal
of his prisoners, that he had already decided
upon.

After a brief but animated discussion, it
was decided to effect their capture by a ruse
which could be put into effect the day be-

fore the ship was ready to sail, when Rowley
was to come ashore to attend a feast to be
given in his honour, and to be preceded by
his payment of the natives for the assistance
they had rendered. Old Potiri, whose
hawk-like eyes were shining with excitement in anticipation of the rich reward he
would receive for his treachery to Rowley,
would not have objected to have had everyone on board ruthlessly slaughtered, had
Kingston suggested it; but promised faith-
fully that no unnecessary violence should
be used. Then one by one, as they had
entered, the natives filed out of the house,
and returned to the principal village, leaving Kingston alone. As he walked down
to the beach, he saw Vailavea sitting under
the shade of a pandanus tree. She rose
and met him.

"Am I as nothing?" she asked him
tremblingly. "Wilt thou not take me with
thee?"

Kingston took her hand. "I cannot,

Vailavea. The country whither I go is far, far from here, and thou wouldst perish among strangers."

"I shall perish of sorrow without thee," she said, gently pushing away his hand, and with bent head she walked sadly away from him without uttering another word.

CHAPTER IX.

THE *Jalasco* was ready for sea again. All her guns, stores, and water were aboard; the hides, closely steeved in the lower hold, made on their upper layer a surface as smooth as a board; and aloft she was as spick and span as a new pin.

It was ten o'clock in the morning, and the captain's boat was alongside ready to take him on shore. A second boat, that which had been stove-in at the island in the Paumotu group, and was now repaired, was on the port side, and loaded with the articles promised to the natives by Rowley.

From the shore came the clamour of many voices. Natives could be seen hurrying to and fro among the houses of the main village, and carrying baskets of food to the *fale kaupule*, or council house, where the captain was to be entertained, and every now and then a conch shell would sound a deep, weirdly-resonant note.

On the deck of the brig everything was in order, and Merrill, who was awaiting the captain's appearance, kept glancing up aloft with a sailor's pride—and he was a born sailor man—at the trim spars, with the neatly furled sails tapering gracefully from their carefully smoothed and rounded bunts to each slender yardarm end. This effect had been achieved, however, principally by himself and Kingston (although the latter had deemed it a work of supererogation); for the crew were, as poor black Worcester used to say, "fine men in a watch below, sah; but not much use in handling a sail, except for spreading it out to lie down and sleep upon."

Kingston, his heart beating high with expectation of what the next hour or two would bring forth, but outwardly calm and indifferent, was on the poop, studiously sewing at a new foretopgallant staysail. Rowley had pressed him to come ashore, but he had declined, saying—what was absolutely true—that he had plenty of work to do on board before the brig lifted her anchor again.

Soon after ten, Rowley came on deck. He was dressed with some degree of care; his always florid face was more florid than usual, and it was very evident that he was highly elated.

"I'm sorry you won't come ashore with me," he said to Kingston; "there will be a lot of fun. There will be a big dance of about three hundred young men and women, and I've promised the chief that after all the junketing is over on shore as many people as we have room for can come aboard, and we'll fire the guns for 'em. Get everything ready, Mr. Merrill; give each gun a double blank charge, rammed well home, and have

11

the muzzles well greased—Portugee nigger fashion—to make a big noise."

"You'll find such a lot of people on the decks a great nuisance," said Kingston, with apparent indifference; "as it is, a lot of canoes are sure to be coming off, crowded with natives, bringing their farewell presents of food and other gear, while you are ashore."

"Oh, well, we must try and put up with 'em," remarked Rowley; "it won't do to offend 'em at the last moment."

"No, I suppose we'll have to put up with them," said Kingston, in a tone of discontent; "but our decks will be in a pretty mess after we get clear of them—pigs, alive and dead, greasy fish, and baskets of food, and all such stuff will make the ship look like a pigstye."

This remark freed Merrill's mind of the very last vestige of doubt concerning Kingston. He was now certain that he was as eager as Rowley and himself to leave the island, and at any moment was likely to come to them and announce his determination to 'stand in' with them. But still he could not help wondering if he (Kingston) would or would not say anything to the captain about the girl Vailavea.

Rowley stepped into his own boat, which was manned by four hands, and, accompanied by the other containing his presents for the natives, pulled ashore, leaving on board his two officers and seven men.

Of these seven, only the sentry on the topgallant foc'sc'le was armed with a carbine and cutlass, although the rest carried their knives in their belts. The mate, as Kingston knew, habitually carried a pistol; and aft on the poop-deck, where their many native visitors were never allowed more than half a dozen at a time, there were always kept ten or a dozen carbines, loaded and capped, and ready for instant use, except that they were concealed from view by a couple of hammocks spread over them in case of rain, and to prevent the heavy night dews from rusting them. Every morning these carbines were carefully examined by Merrill, who had several times fired and re-loaded them since they had been placed there; and Kingston could not but admire the man's continuous caution, even when there appeared to be not the slightest necessity for it.

Rowley had twice suggested that these arms should be taken below or put entirely out of sight, as their presence implied a distrust of the natives, and was likely to be a cause of offence, if not resentment, but Merrill had protested strongly, and appealed to Kingston for his opinion, and the latter, for reasons of his own, of course, sided with the mate and said it would be as well to leave them where they were.

"Just so," said Merrill. "Guess we should look pretty sick if a muss did occur, and we were cut off from access to the poop. The men can't work about the deck carrying guns, but they know where to get them if they do want them."

An hour after Rowley had gone ashore, Kingston was still sewing at the staysail; Merrill was engaged with two or three of the men in re-stowing a few small articles in the lazzarette, and the rest of the crew were at various tasks on deck. Suddenly the sound of a chorus of many voices came from the shore, and rising to his feet, the second officer saw a long procession of natives of both sexes marching down from the village to the boats.

"Tell Senor Merrill to come on deck," he said to one of the men; "one of the boats is coming off with a lot of canoes."

Merrill came on deck, and looked at the approaching boat, which was crowded with natives, and was accompanied by eight or ten canoes. He could see that there were a number of women in both canoes and boat, and as they came paddling towards the ship they sang melodiously together.

Kingston went below with leisurely step. Once inside his cabin, he put on his coat, thrust a loaded pistol in the breast pocket, then returned to the poop, and, with the unsuspecting Merrill, awaited the arrival of the visitors.

The boat came alongside first. She was deeply laden with baskets of cooked food— such as fish, pork, bread fruit, and taro—all of which were passed up on deck. Then the occupants of the boat, some twenty or more of native men and women, followed. The boat was then veered astern, and the canoes, each of which was manned by four or five stalwart men, and contained live pigs and fowls, came to the side, and the natives clambered on deck, laughing and singing and apparently bent on enjoying themselves.

In a few minutes they were fraternising with the crew, two of them, with several young girls, going up on the topgallant foc'sc'le to the armed sentry, and placing a basket of young drinking coconuts at his feet. Fonu, who was in charge of the party, came aft with another native and ascended to the poop, where he engaged in conversation with the two officers.

"When is the captain coming off?" asked Merrill.

"Very soon," replied the native, who, nonchalantly filling his pipe, was eagerly awaiting an opportunity to whisper a word to Kingston. It soon came.

"I daresay the women would like some biscuits, Fonu," said Merrill. "I'll tell the steward."

The moment he was out of sight, Fonu turned to Kingston.

"We are ready. See, close beside every sailor are two or three of our men. When *you* are ready I need but call."

"Then be prepared. As soon as I fling my arms around the mate, you know what to do; first, *saisai le gutu*" (gag. him), "and then tie his hands behind his back. Here

is cord," and he handed him some small
line. "Now, follow me."

He turned and descended into the cabin.
Merrill was standing near the table, watching the steward putting piles of biscuits on
the cabin table. He was about to move
aside to let his subordinate pass, when
Kingston suddenly threw his arms around
him in a vice-like grip.

"You are my prisoner, Mr. Merrill."

Ere the astonished officer could utter a
word, Fonu had gagged him effectually with
a strip of soft, beaten bark; and the terrified
steward was seized by the throat by a second
native, who held a knife to his heart. He
submitted to be gagged without a murmur.

"Attempt to move, and you are dead
men," said Kingston to the prisoners as
they were marched along to the end of the
main cabin. "This man" (and he pointed
to the grim, nude warrior who had seized the
steward) "will kill you the moment you
make the slightest noise."

He stooped and examined the lashings on their hands; then going to his cabin returned with a carpenter's broad axe—a fearful looking weapon—which he placed in the hand of the native, with a significant gesture, and said something to him in his own tongue.

"I don't want to hurt you, Merrill," he said earnestly, "but I implore you if you value your life not to let this man think you meditate freeing yourself. I have told him to cut you down without mercy, if you move. In five minutes I will take that brutal gag off."

In another instant he was gone, with faithful Fonu at his heels. The moment they gained the poop, the laughter and sounds of merriment on the main deck seemed to cease, as if by magic, and the crew looked up in wonder. Then Fonu, stepping to the break of the poop, clapped his hands.

In a moment a score of natives threw

themselves upon the seamen, and without a cry they were overpowered and bound.

"Down into the hold with them," cried Kingston, as he tore off the hammocks from the carbines on the poop, and passed them to a dozen natives, who followed the prisoners below with instructions to fell the first man who made any effort to free himself.

Then he darted to the signal locker, took out the brig's colours, and hoisted them at the gaff. It was the signal he had agreed upon with Potiri to announce the recapture of the ship. A loud, sonorous shout from five hundred throats answered it, and he knew that Rowley and his men were being made prisoners.

Then, again attended by Fonu and some of the natives, he re-entered the cabin, and went into Merrill's state room, from which he took a dozen pair of handcuffs—all that were on board. Throwing ten pair on the table, he came up to the mate, cut the lashing which bound his hands, and cut the gag.

"All the crew who are on board are prisoners; so, by this time, is Captain Rowley and those with him. The ship is in my hands. I am sorry I had to gag you, but it could not be helped. Now I shall have to put these on."

Merrill quietly held out his hands for the handcuffs. "You've done the thing smartly, I must say. But you needn't ornament me with these bracelets. I give in."

Kingston shook his head. "I believe you—but I must be careful. Rowley will be here to keep you company presently; and until I get clear of you both, I must keep you in irons."

"Just so," said the imperturbable American, without the slightest anger in his voice or manner; "but I'd like to think out over a cigar why I was such a blazing idiot. There's a pile on my table."

Kingston brought him a couple of cigars,

and Merrill, raising his manacled hands, lit one from a match held by his captor, and puffed it contentedly.

"You needn't put the matches in your pocket on my account," he drawled. "I'm not big enough fool to try to do any mischief with them. Reckon Rowley won't like this turn up any more than I do. Are you going to leave anyone here to minister to my wants in the way of liquid refreshment during these interesting proceedings?"

Kingston, admiring the man's equanimity, laughed, went to the sideboard, poured some brandy into a glass, added water, and himself handed it to Merrill. Then he went on deck, just as the captain's boat, now manned by natives, came alongside, with Rowley and the four seamen who had gone ashore with him, securely bound.

They were at once brought on board, and something like pity came into Kingston's heart when he saw Rowley's face, and met his glance. For the moment he did not speak to him, but motioned to Fonu to cut the thin lashing of cinnet which bound his hands and feet.

" I have no choice but to put handcuffs on you, Captain Rowley," he said ; " the ship is mine now, and the mate and all the crew are prisoners. I am taking her back to Valparaiso."

Rowley made no answer. He seemed half-dazed, for he had made a desperate resistance and it had taken half a dozen men to overpower him when old Potiri had given the signal for him to be seized. However, he went below quietly, and was placed beside Merrill. A number of natives stood over them on guard.

Then presently, moved by a not unnatural sentiment of pity, Kingston had them both taken into the cuddy, where they could not see and hear what was to follow—i.e., the reception in the main cabin of old Potiri and the head men, and the handing over to them of the various articles promised by Kingston.

This was a task of nearly an hour, although, to get it over as quickly as possible, Kingston liberated the steward and two of the seamen in the hold. He scrupulously fulfilled his promises to the natives, and soon after noon, old Potiri and a number of natives, after bidding him a warm farewell, left the brig in half a dozen deeply laden canoes.

Another hour passed, during which time the two prisoners in the cuddy heard the sound of much preparation going on on deck, and then suddenly Rowley said gaspingly to Merrill—" By heavens, I believe he's getting under weigh. I hear the windlass."

Merrill nodded, but made no answer, and Rowley bent his head upon his chest, and gave himself up to his own bitter reflections. Then they heard Kingston come into the cabin, where he remained for some time, evidently very busy.

Presently the cuddy door was opened, and

Kingston entered, followed by Fonu and some of the islanders. Without speaking, he went up to Rowley and unlocked his handcuffs.

"Come into the cabin," he said quietly but firmly.

One brief glance at the throng of armed natives who all but filled the main cabin showed the captain that resistance meant death.

"Sit down, please," said Kingston, trying not to speak with unnecessary harshness, for he really pitied Rowley when he looked at him—the man seemed to have aged suddenly.

They sat down and waited for their captor to speak.

"As I told you, I am taking this brig to Valparaiso, and, by God's help, I hope to re-establish my name as an honest man. If I did my full duty, I would keep you both —and the crew as well—in irons until we reached there, when I could hand you all over to the proper authorities. But I cannot reconcile myself to the idea of keeping anyone in irons on such a long voyage as is before me. Neither could I liberate you. I shall have to beat against the south-east trades for at least a thousand miles before I get a slant that will enable me to reach the coast of South America. I have no one on board but natives to work the ship. And you, as well as I do, know what it would mean to you if I did take you back."

Neither of them answered, though Rowley heaved a quick, gasping sigh.

"Now this is what I have decided to do," resumed Kingston. "I have fitted out the longboat in such a manner that she will easily carry you and all the crew anywhere up to a thousand miles. She is provided with a month's provisions and water, and I am giving you a sextant, chart, and the best boat compass on board. Neither of you are navigators?"

Rowley shook his head.

"Well, that doesn't matter. Ninety miles south-west from this island is Funafuti. It is a big island, and you can't possibly miss it. There are one or two white men living there, and the place is well known to the American whaling flet. Ships touch there pretty frequently. What you do after you get there doesn't matter to me. I daresay you can spin as likely a yarn as you spun me in Arica."

"Go ahead with your discourse," said Merrill, "but cut it as short as you can."

Kingston nodded. "I'll make it as short as I can, I assure you, for the sooner we are clear of each other, the better I'll like it."

Then he pointed to a pile of articles on the cabin table.

"I've gone through both of your cabins, and have had all your private effects taken out. In your cabin, Captain Rowley, I found some money which I suppose

12

belongs to you — about three thousand dollars ? "

" It's mine," said Rowley, sullenly.

" Well, there it is. And with it is the five hundred dollars you advanced me in Arica ; that sum I took out of the sixty thousand dollars belonging to Moreno Brothers. Whether I am doing wrong or not, I have not time to consider, but anyway there is your money. All your gear, Merrill, is there also—money, papers and clothing."

" You are a right good sort of Britisher," said the American, " and I wish you luck."

Unheeding the interruption, Kingston resumed.

" I am giving you six carbines and plenty of ammunition, in case you might need arms ; you will find the powder and ball headed up in a water breaker. The boat is so fitted and so well found, that you could keep to sea for a couple of months if you

had to do so. But if you steer S.W. you'll
be in Funafuti Lagoon in forty-eight hours
after you leave here. You have a good
compass—the best I can spare. Now that
is all. You can get your gear together and
start in ten minutes. The boat is alongside,
all ready."

A quarter of an hour later, Rowley,
Merrill and the crew of the *Jalasco*
descended into the boat and pushed off.
Merrill alone made a sign of farewell to
Kingston, who answered it with a wave of
his hand. In half an hour they were
outside the reef, and hoisting the fore
and aft mainsail and jib, stood away for
Funafuti.

Long afterwards Kingston heard that
they reached the island safely, and from
there went to Japan in a New Bedford
whaler. What became of them eventually
he never heard.

Long ere the boat was out of sight there

was renewed activity on board the *Jalasco*, for her new crew of wild, excited islanders, aided by scores of their countrymen, had hove-short her cable, and now with her top-sails hoisted and sheeted home, she strained gently at her anchor, buried deep in the coral forest below, as if anxious to be once more slapping the swelling seas aside with her sharp cutwater.

Kingston, pacing to and fro on the poop, watched the last of the shore-going natives descend into their canoes. All round the ship were scores of other canoes, filled with people who had come to say farewell to Fonu and the new crew, but in none of them could he discern the figure of the girl whom he knew loved him. He called Fonu aft.

" Why did not she come to bid me good-bye ? " he asked.

Fonu made a peculiar gesture with his hand, as of one who wishes to put aside the discussion of a sorrowful subject.

"She would be ashamed to come here and weep before so many," he said, simply. "Many of her friends will weep with her when we are gone—others may but laugh at her."

Kingston bent his head, but made no reply.

Then he drew himself together, and cried out sharply—

"Heave away, boys."

And with a wild cry, which was taken up by the people in the canoes surrounding the brig, the waiting crew sprang to the windlass, and as the anchor lifted, the *Jalasco* canted off to starboard, and under topsails and staysails only, began to slip over the smooth waters of the lagoon towards the passage through the reef, Fonu and three or four of his countrymen working like tigers to get the anchor aboard and secured in seamanlike fashion.

. Once outside the passage, Kingston hauled to the wind, and let the brig run

close along the roaring line of leaping surf
on the barrier reef till he was abreast of the
village, for the islet of Teanamu, on which
it stood, was so narrow that the houses
could be seen from either the inside of the
lagoon, or from the ocean on the western
side.

As the brig backed her main yard and
lay gracefully dipping her sharp bows into
the ocean swell just beyond the white line
of surf, the whole population of the atoll
gathered together under the line of waving
palms fringing the shore, and a mighty
shout came from nearly a thousand throats
as her ten guns bellowed out a farewell
salute.

And then the *Jalasco* filled again, and
stood away on her long, long voyage towards the rising sun.

On the fourteenth day out from Nukufetau,
Danger Island was sighted, and running in
close to the reef, Kingston hove-to and fired
a gun. A fleet of canoes shot out from the

lagoon, and the first man to board the brig
was José Pimental, who almost wept with
joy and excitement as he sprang towards
the captain, and embraced him in his im-
pulsive fashion. And then once more the
Jalasco turned to the east.

.   .   .   .

Early one morning, and nearly eight
weeks after those on board the brig had
seen the low line of palms on Nukufetau
sink below the horizon, two men were
galloping over a country road ten miles
from Valparaiso. One was Kingston's storekeeper friend, the other was Kingston himself. Presently they came to a little noisy
stream, and drew rein. Half a mile away
they could discern the roof of Captain
Forestier's house, showing through the trees.

"Come, let us push on," said Kingston's
friend; "we must get there before they go
to breakfast."

They rode straight up the wide path to
the door, and the first man to see them was

the old merchant. He was standing in the porch, smoking his cigar. His stern grey eyes lit up with amazement when he saw who was one of the visitors.

Kingston jumped off his horse.

"Just come ashore, sir," he said politely, touching his hat; "the *Jalasco* is in port, safe and sound."

"Come inside," said Forestier huskily, as he held out both his hands. "God knows you are welcome, even had you come without my ship, which I never expected to hear of again."

He drew them inside quietly to his study, and closed the door, and for half an hour they remained together, whilst Kingston related his strange, eventful story.

Then Captain Forestier, with misty eyes, went to his daughter's bedroom.

"Rosa, dear. Come here, I want you."

"What is it, father, dear?" and Rosa Forestier, pale and sad, opened the door languidly.

"Go to my room, my dear," said the old man, kissing her tenderly; " there is someone waiting for you—someone whom you love dearly, and whom I shall be proud to call my daughter's husband."

'Mulholland kicked him on the hand with such violence that he broke
several of the small bones.''

[*See page* 189.

'HOPE'

A MEMORY OF 'BULLY' HAYES

A BIG, stern-faced man with bright blue eyes, and a long snow-white beard was sitting on a native bench outside a house which stood on the western point of Utwe Harbour.[1] He was looking at the topmasts of a vessel sunk in five fathoms of water, and as he gazed he sighed, for the torn and shattered hull that lay upon the coral bottom had once been the joy of his heart.

The man was Captain Hayes—'Bully' Hayes, everyone called him—and the wrecked vessel was the famous and beautiful lily-

[1] Port Lottin on Kûsaie (Strong's Island), one of the Caroline Group.

white brig *Leonora,* dashed on the reef one
wild, black night in March four months
before.   And Hayes next morning was a
ruined man, hard set to keep in control his
motley ship's company of ninety-three people
—white men, savage islanders from the
equatorial Pacific, and cut-throat half-breeds
and mongrels hailing from all ports, from
the Golden Gate to Valdivia and the Chiloe
Islands.

But reckless and dissolute as were the
majority of the crew and passengers of the
ill-fated brig, the mad license in which they
at first indulged when they found themselves
freed from the authority of their grim,
passionate captain, did not last long.   For
Hayes was a man of iron resolution and
dauntless courage—a man who was born to
lead and command not a gathering of broken
ruffians and scoundrels, as had always been
his evil fate, but men bent upon some noble
enterprise or deed of daring.   Singling out
those men—white and coloured—who, in the

wild excitement following the wreck of his
ship, had defied his authority—he challenged
them individually and collectively to fight.
Only two responded—his chief mate (a man
named Nahnsen) and a trader, one Harry
Mulholland, an American.

Nahnsen, a brutal, ill-tempered Dane, was
a man of enormous strength, and stood six
feet two inches in his stockinged feet. But
he had no idea of using his hands, and when
Hayes knocked him down in the first round,
he drew a Derringer pistol from his hip
pocket as he lay on the sand, and pointed it
at his opponent, when Mulholland, awaiting
his 'turn' with the redoubtable 'Bully,'
kicked him on the hand with savage contempt. Hayes looked at the prostrate man
with cool indifference, picked up the pistol,
put it in his pocket, and then called him an
ungrateful hound—not fit to associate with
white men. Then as the Dane slunk away
amid the jeers of the very men who had pro-
fessed their willingness to stand by him, the

captain turned to Mulholland and asked him
if *he* was ready.

"No," was the frank reply; "I guess you
and I had best shake hands."

This ended what would certainly have
led to mutiny and bloodshed, and Hayes,
who had a wonderful tact at times, soon
won back the men's allegiance. Within a
week he had them all at work for him,
building houses for themselves, their wives
and children, and their wild following of
Pleasant Islanders; making coco-nut oil, boat-
building, and other employments. It was
his intention to accumulate such a quantity
of oil that he hoped that at the end of
twelve months he would be able to charter
a whaleship to take him to either Samoa
or his secret rendezvous in the north-west
—Arrecifos or Providence Islands—a chain
of islets enclosing a magnificent lagoon.
Here he intended to manufacture oil on an
extensive scale, for the islands were covered
with thousands of coco-palms, and had but

a score of its own numerous inhabitants remaining. Two years before, when he first entered the lagoon, he had discovered these people, gained their friendship, and taken possession of their territory, leaving two white men in charge. With a hundred or so imported labourers from the Gilbert group and Ocean and Pleasant Islands to work for him, he had every reason to believe that in a very few years he would become a wealthy man.

And so the months went by, and the famous captain was well content, as he saw, day by day, cask after cask of oil added to others in the great thatched-roofed shed he had built near his dwelling-house. But as time went on, some of the white men again began to plot against him, but secretly, and with fear and trembling for their lives, for he was a man to be dreaded when in anger, and two of the plotters had, on Raven Island, one day seen him strike a man dead with a single blow. So they set to work quietly, and Hayes, if he suspected, made no sign. The King of Kusaie, though openly professing the greatest friendship for the captain, both hated and feared him; for Hayes, in an evil moment of temper, had treated some of the leading natives with harshness amounting to cruelty, charging them with having incited their people to steal a number of valuable articles from the wreck. Then, too, Sé, the queen, was a young and handsome woman, and Tokusā, the king, was old and wizened, and even his own subjects whispered and laughed when they spoke of Hayes and the young queen. And so the king sent secret words of encouragement to the plotters, and with his chiefs waited for the time to strike, and rid the island of their oppressor and his dreaded and savage native crew—men whose ferocious aspect terrified the Kusaieans, and who stole their youngest and prettiest women, and laughed when the king sent a deputation to Hayes and asked him to

restore them. For they knew what the
big man would say :

"If a woman is worth having, she is
worth fighting for," he said to the king's
messengers. "Go back and tell the king
that this is a thing that does not concern
me, and I shall not interfere. And yet, if
the lovers or husbands of these women whom
the king says have been stolen, come here to
fight with the robbers, they shall have a
fair field, and I shall see that no advantage
is taken of them—even if I kill the best
man of all my crew."

But the men of Kusaie knew they were
no match for the tough, herculean-limbed
Pleasant Islanders, and so the messengers
went back disappointed to the king at
Lelé, and the hatred to Hayes deepened
day by day. Still he made no sign.

And every day, when the sun dipped
over the crest of Mont Buaché, he would
come and sit outside his great house and
watch his crew and the other natives bath-
13

ing in the surf after their toil). Sometimes, when his mood was pleasant, he would be surrounded by many people, laughing and jesting with them all—from the oldest white trader to toddling whitey-brown infants. But when he sat alone and gazed at the spars of the sunken brig, there were but few who dared to disturb him then, for they well knew that he was lost in his own thoughts, and brooding in sullen resentment over his misfortunes.

But on this day there sat with him two persons—the only two perhaps of all his ship's company for whom he really cared; the only two. whom he had not at some time or other turned upon with a savage oath or a threat. One was his supercargo, a man whom he knew he could neither corrupt nor threaten, and consequently thought highly of him; the other was ' Hope.'

Hope was only a little native boy of ten years of age, with a skin like polished copper-bronze, and eyes like the sea when it lies calm and sleeping under myriad stars. His hair, wavy and black as night, fell upon his square, sturdy little shoulders, and as he looked up into the grim, bearded face of his master and friend, and laughed, his white teeth shone like pearl.

Hayes put his hand on the child's head.

"Why don't you go and bathe, you lazy little beggar?"

Hope laughed in his childish, merry treble. He understood and spoke English well, but answered in his native tongue, rolling and guttural.

"I will stay here with thee, capitan. Thou saidst thou wouldst walk on the reef to-day, and that I should bring my fish-spear."

Hayes shook his head. "I am too tired to-day, Hope. To-morrow, perhaps."

But the child persisted, and Hayes yielded, and he rose and walked down towards the reef (which was exposed and dry, for the tide was low), and the boy trotted beside him, brandishing a dainty little fish spear, made from a bit of the wrecked brig's ironwork.

The supercargo watched them with a certain feeling of annoyance, for he much desired to speak to the captain on a matter of importance to himself, and had been but waiting a favourable opportunity — as soon as Hayes' gloomy fit had left him — and now he and the boy would probably remain on the reef until sunset.

" After all, however," thought the supercargo, as he filled his pipe again, " it is just as well. I daresay Hope's chatter and antics will put him in a good temper by another half hour. And I don't want to have a row on the last evening I shall spend here."

Presently there came up to the supercargo and sat down on the ground beside him a young, full-blooded negro seaman— a man whom the supercargo liked for his careless good-nature, and for his freedom from the vices and villainy with which

most of his shipmates were so plentifully
endowed.

"De ole man's mighty fond of dat Hope,.
sah," he said, 'pointing' with his chin
towards the reef.

"Yes, Sam. Hope is 'the white-headed
boy' with the captain. There's no mis-
take about that. And he's a good little
fellow; but the women are spoiling him,
and the young monkey fancies he can do
anything he likes."

"Dat's so," and the negro laughed. "He
came to me yes'day, an' sez, 'Sam, jest
you lend me yo' Winchester rifle.' 'What
fo'? I sez. 'Oh, on'y to *faiaga* (play)
with,' sez he. So I jest jerks out de twelve
cartridges and han's him de Winchester.
Den off he goes, smilin' all over. And den
in 'bout ten minutes, I hears a bang! bang!
bang! three times ober dar by de oil shed.
So off I runs, an' dar was dat boy shootin'
at de captain's pigs in one of de pens. One
ob dem was stone dead, too."

"The young villain!" said the supercargo. "I thought I missed eight of my
own cartridges some days ago!"

"Dat's so, sah. He bin tole me he
found 'em in your gun bag. I took away
de other five an' tole him I was jes' goin'
right away to tell you 'bout it. Den somehow he sorter got roun' me, an' I promised
not to tell you. Here dey are, sah."

The supercargo took the cartridges and
dropped them into the pocket of his
pyjamas jacket. "I thought the young
beggar was unusually quiet to-day—now I
know the reason."

"I bin tole, sah, dat de reason de ole
man cottons to de chile so much is dat he
killed his father."

"That is quite true, but it was hardly
the captain's fault. It was at Hope
Island in the Kingsmill group that it
happened, about nine years ago."

Then he told the negro the story.

"The captain had had a quarrel with a

white trader there named Jack Rudd,
and they had fought. Rudd was badly
hurt, and told the natives that when
Hayes came on shore again he meant to
shoot him. Someone came off on board
and told .the skipper, who took it very
quietly, and said that he was pretty sure
Jack Rudd would take mighty good care
to hide himself in a safe place before 'he
did any shooting. That was exactly what
he did do. He hid inside his boat-house,
intending to fire at the captain as he was
going past. But a native named Bari, who
used to do odd jobs of work for Rudd,
slipped away from his house quietly, so as
to warn the captain. Unfortunately the
poor fellow took a loaded rifle with him,
meaning to give it to the captain, who he
thought might come on shore unarmed,
and be shot down. It so happened that
when he did land, almost the first thing he
saw was a native, crouched down behind
a bush, with a gun in his hand, and imagin-

ing it was someone waiting to take a pot
shot at him, he drew his pistol and fired
and smashed Bari's hip bone. Before he
could fire again, however, Rudd made a
bolt out of the boat-shed, and the captain
went after him. But Rudd got safely away
into the bush, and when the skipper came
back and heard poor Bari's story, he did
all for him that possibly could be done—
brought him on board, and nursed him
until he died, a month afterwards. Bari's
wife and child came on board the ship with
him, and when he died, the captain coaxed
her to give the boy to him, and he's been
with him ever since. He was named 'Hope
Hayes' by the skipper. That's the yarn."

"Guess de ole man hes a pow'ful soft
spot in his heart fo' de chile," said the negro;
"wish his han' was as soft sometimes. De
fust time he hit me it felt like if fo' or five
mules hed kicked me all together in de one
place."

The supercargo smiled and nodded, and

then limped away (for he was lame from an injury he had received·when the brig was wrecked) to his own quarters—a small roughly-built house of one room, situated between the captain's dwelling-house and the boat-sheds on the lagoon side of the settlement. On the walls and on a raised bed of canework were his few possessions— all that had been saved from the wreck—a repeating rifle, a shot gun, fishing tackle, a harpoon, and some odds and ends of 'trade,' such as knives, beads, printed calico, a few handkerchiefs, and a small case of tobacco.

" Not much to begin housekeeping with," he said, as he surveyed his belongings, "'but many a man has started worse off than that in the South Seas."

Closing the door, as he did not wish to be interrupted, he took a native mat, rolled up in it all the articles it could contain, and tied it up neatly with some coir cinnet, then laid the guns and other things beside it, all in readiness.

Stepping outside in the now fast fading daylight, he pulled to the door, and looked towards the roof. Hayes and the boy were returning. He walked down to the beach, and seating himself on a coral boulder, waited.

"Hallo," said the captain cheerily in his deep tones, "come to lend a hand to carry up the fish?" and he pointed to a fish a few inches long impaled on Hope's spear.

The supercargo smiled at the boy—then motioned to Hayes to sit down. "I want to talk to you, captain, if you please. And we can talk here better than up there," and he nodded towards three or four white men, who were now walking to and fro on the sandy plaza in front of the captain's house, waiting for the steward's supper bell.

"What is it?" and as 'Bully' sat down he bent his keen blue eyes on the young man's face.

Now the supercargo, though he had many quarrels with his captain, and hated some of the things he had done, yet liked the man sincerely, and he found it hard to say that which he had come to say. So he hesitated and sought for words, but none came. Then he stood up and held out his hand.

"I have come to say good-bye. Let us part friends."

Hayes sprang to his feet, placed his two hands on the young man's shoulders, and forced him to resume his seat. When he spoke, it was very quietly.

"I'm not going to let you go away like this. . . . I'm not going to let you go away at all. I never thought you would leave me in the lurch."

"I am not leaving you in the lurch, captain. And I am sorry to go ; but go I must."

"I know you are dissatisfied with some things that have occurred. But let it pass. You are the only man I can trust. And, by God, I have always acted squarely with you."

"With me—yes. But I'm full of—of some things. And I'm deadly sick of living here day after day, sick of the eternal quarrels and fights and blood-letting in which l should have no concern. And this last matter has wound me up, captain."

"You mean about those Kusaiean women?"

The supercargo nodded. "Yes, what else? For God's sake have some pity on the poor creatures, and send them back to the king. Do you know that two of them ran away from the men to whom you gave them, and have been hiding in the mangroves for a day and a night, and that that damned scoundrel Manuel, with a dozen swine like him, are looking for them now?"

An angry gleam came into the blue eyes.

"Send them back? I'll neither send them back, nor let them go back." He laughed savagely—"They shall stay here—'captives to the bow and spear' of my trusty blackguards, and if old King Tokusā tries to play a double game with me, he'll find his darned old thatched-roof palace ablaze over his head. By——I'll burn the whole town and drive him and his people into the bush."

"I don't doubt that you would; but I don't think you would drive that little she-devil of a Sé very far away from you. As it is, I wonder she has not been set up in business as a queen at Utwe already."

Hayes laughed. He was as vain as a child in some things. Then speaking very earnestly, he tried to induce the supercargo to remain with the rest of the ship's company; for apart from the real regard he had for the young man, he had another motive—that of self-interest. But he did not attempt to disguise it.

"If you leave me, half of the younger fellows—white and brown—will desert and follow you. That will be hard lines on me."

"Harder on me, captain. I don't want them. And what is more, I won't have them. The village where I am going to live is only a small bit of a place, and none of the people are too beastly fond of any of the crowd from the *Leonora*."

"Oh, well, I suppose you are going to make yourself more comfortable," said Hayes with something like a sneer, for again his evil temper was rising.

"Looks like it, doesn't it! All my gear, including a small box of tobacco and a Winchester, isn't worth two hundred dollars. And I'm going to live in a native house with natives, and feed and sleep like a native, because I can't afford to live like a white man."

"That means that you want your money," was the captain's sullen comment; "come up to the house, then, and we'll square up."

"When I want it, I'll ask for it. But I shall be glad of a bag of shot, some powder and caps. You have plenty."

"You can take what you want."

"Thanks. I'll send someone for it, and the rest of my gear in a few minutes. I'll go on ahead." Then once more he held out his hand.

"Good-bye, Hayes."

"Good-bye."

"Let Hope come and stay with me a day sometimes."

"I won't promise. Good-bye."

And so the redoubtable 'Bully' and his supercargo parted.

.   .   .   .   .   .

Three months had passed. The supercargo, now recovered from his lameness, was sitting under the shady verandah of a native house, endeavouring to patch the remnants of a pair of boots with some worn-out ship's pump-leather. Hope, who had just come from a walk to the river near by, was squatted on his heels near him, watching the operation with intense earnestness.

Two days before he had come to the

village, escorted by Black Sam, who bore
a note from Hayes :

. "Master Hope has been in mischief again. I had nine
turtle in the pond. The young villain opened the gate at
high tide, and let 'em· out. Keep him with you till
Thursday."

"Do you know that you're going back
to Utwe to-morrow, you young ruffian ?"
said the supercargo, as he drilled a hole
through the piece of leather he held.

Hope nodded, shrugged his shoulders with
a martyr-like air, and then pretended to see
something very interesting up in the roof.

"Glad to go back ? "

"No" (with indifference).

"Well, you *are* going back—that's
certain. What is that you have there
inside your jumper ? It's moving."

"Only an eel."

"An eel ! Show it to me."

Hope took·out a round wet bundle of
red twill, about the size of a husked coco-
nut, and put it down on the verandah.

Through the thin cloth the form of the
hideous fish could be seen squirming and
wriggling in its efforts to escape.

"What did you bring the dirty *toan*
here for? And from where the piece of
red cloth?"

"I took it from another boy. It was
his waist cloth, and I gave him a tin of
powder for it."

"A tin of powder!" exclaimed the man,
"Who gave you a tin of powder?"

"You did," replied the boy, in English,
with such an irresistible air of gravity
that his questioner looked at him in astonishment.

"*I* did?"

"Yes, you gave me the *tin*."

"And who the powder?"

"I made it."

"*You* made it. How? Where?"

"This morning. I gathered a lot of
charcoal from the cook-house, and beat it
into a fine dust and filled the tin with it.

14

Then when I went to bathe in the river, I met some boys and asked them to catch a *toan* for me.   Then "—here he began to speak with the most alarming rapidity— "one of them said it was unlucky for anyone to touch a *toan*, but he would catch one for me if I gave him my tin of powder.   And . . . . and he said he would give me his waist cloth to tie it up in.   It will never die, will a *toan*, if the devil which is in it gets water put on its eyes twice when the moon is young. - So *he* caught the *toan*, and tied it up in the cloth, and *I* gave him the tin of powder."

"Hope," and the supercargo tried hard to look stern, "you are a bad boy.   It was not powder."

"*I* did not say it was powder," he said meekly.   "*He* said it was powder."

The white man turned his face aside to hide a smile.   Then—

"I don't like boys who tell lies, or cheat.

And you are a cheat. Now, see, I meant to take you back to the captain myself to-morrow, but now I shall send you back with some one else."

In an instant the boy's dark eyes filled. "Don't do that. I am sorry, very sorry. And I did not mean to cheat. Ah, Tuhi" (the supercargo's native name), "*don't* send me back with anyone else. . . . The captain said you *might* come back with me and stay at Utwe again."

'Tuhi,' who loved the child, relented. "Very well. I'll take you back. But you must throw away that eel."

Hope's face fell, and his lips twitched—"I promised to take it to Utwe."

"Promised whom ?"

"Sebat, the Pleasant Island witchwoman. She will take its eyes out, and put them into the mate's food; then he will sicken and die. And he is a bad man, and hates the captain, and so I promised."

The supercargo took the bundle, carried

it down to the beach, and threw it into
the water. Hope's eyes filled, and then
two big tears coursed down his brown cheeks.

"You must not do what Sebat tells you
without first asking the captain. And it is
a wrong and wicked thing that she has
asked you to do ; it would have angered the
captain greatly. Now I shall work no
more to-day. Get your fishing rod and
come with me, and we shall catch some
lupo (gar-fish) for our supper."

In a moment the black eyes beamed with
delight, for the little fellow had the soul of
a true sportsman, and nothing could exceed
his joy when his white friend took him
fishing on the reef or lagoon, or shooting on
the mountains. At picking up and following the tracks of a wild pig he was a
marvel of skill and patience, and 'Tuhi'
was always glad of his company, for the
spirit of mischief that always animated the
boy in his idle moments left him the
moment he was in a canoe, or was stealing

silently through the forest trees, his keen eyes bent upon the leafy carpet that covered the ground, or scanning the branches overhead in search of some sleeping pigeon. Then, no sound beyond a whisper ever escaped his lips.

Before sunrise on the following morning, they started for Utwe, following a mountain path that led into the interior, and traversed the centre of the island, for the white man intended to shoot pigeons on the way. As the sun rose, they halted and ate their simple breakfast of baked bonito and cold yam. Then Hope carefully filled his friend's pipe, and the two struck into the deep forest, the sound of the beating surf behind them growing fainter and fainter as they walked, till at last it was lost altogether, and only the rustle of the tree tops and the soft call of the wood doves broke the silence.

At noon they rested under the shade of a

mighty, many buttressed *kamoian* tree, which grew almost alone on a rocky spur of Mount Crozer; and far below them, they could see Utwe village and the little harbour in which lay the sunken *Leonora*, and beyond that the long wavering line of reef trending eastward, with here and there a spot of white beach facing the tumbling surf. Whilst the supercargo sat with his back against the tree, and smoked and gazed dreamily at the scene before him, Hope plucked a fat pigeon, split it open with his clasp knife, and then proceeded to grill it over a small fire of dried twigs, turning it carefully and solemnly and pursing up his lips when now and then the rich, yellow fat blazed up and made the glowing embers blacken and smoke. Then, when it was cooked, he placed it on a platter of leaves, carefully removing every adhering cinder, and after looking at it critically for a few moments, breathed a sigh of satisfaction.

"Tuhi, thy bird is ready," he said in his mother tongue, which the white man spoke well.

"Eat it yourself, Hope, my boy. I am not hungry."

"Ah, Tuhi!"

The words were uttered so reproachfully, and the speaker looked so disconsolate, that the supercargo laughed, drew the bird to him, and divided it in halves, giving one to the boy, together with a piece of taro brought from the village.

"Thou art a great cook, Hope. Some day when I become a rich man, I shall hire thee to cook for me."

Hope shook his head gravely. "Nay, not for hire, for that would be but the work of a slave. But still if the capitan would let me I should go with thee—not for ever, but for a time."

The supercargo nodded. "I see. Wouldst be a sailor?"

"Aye; but still better would I like to be

a boat-steerer, and kill whales. Hast ever killed a whale, Tuhi?"

"No, but I have seen many killed, for I have pulled in boats."

Hope sighed. "Ah, would I were grown up, and were standing in the bow of a boat with the harpoon in my hand, and then ———" he leant backwards with upraised hands, as would a harpooner when poising his iron.

"I have known some harpooners who, when striking a whale for the first time, have trembled," said the man, slyly.

The boy sniffed contemptuously. "Pah! *I* would not tremble. I am no coward. I am afraid of nothing and no one."

"Not even the captain?"

"Ah! I did not mean *him*; yes, I am afraid of him when he strokes his beard, and his eyes come together, and he speaks thickly."

"So are many people, Hope," said his friend with a laugh. "Now, let us be going, or it will be dark ere we get to the east side of the harbour, and then unless the captain sees us, and sends a boat or a canoe, we shall have to sleep there and be devoured by *namu* (mosquitoes)."

The descent to the sea took them till within an hour of sundown, for pigeons were plentiful that day; and by the time they reached the eastern shore of the harbour, Hope had as many of the fat, heavy birds as he could carry, and the supercargo had a score over his shoulder.

At the base of the mountain, and standing on the margin of a small tidal creek, was an untenanted native house, temporarily abandoned by its former occupants on account of the plague of mosquitoes which swarmed in the dense mangrove jungle around. In front of the house, and covered over by leaves to protect it from the sun, was a very small canoe which had been built to hold either one grown person or two boys. Such tiny craft were used by

the Kusaiean children for crossing in the
smooth waters of the lagoon, and were
quite unfitted for use in rough water.

Hope eyed it, threw off the covering of
branches, and lifted one end.

"'Twould hold us both if we were very
careful, Tuhi," he said suggestively.

'Tuhi' shook his head. "Aye, it would
in smooth water, but 'tis not fit to cross a
mile of the open sea water. It might fill—
and between here and Utwe are many
sharks. Light a fire and make a signal
of smoke."

Hayes had been watching, saw the signal,
and at once had his own favourite boat—
the *Leonora's* twelve-foot dinghy—put into
the water. There was a gentle breeze from
the south-east, and under her mainsail and
jib the little craft slipped away from the
shore, and stood across the passage, which
was nearly a mile in width. A heavy swell
was tumbling through the mouth of the
harbour, and bursting with sullen violence

against a long ledge of reef, stretching out almost into the centre, and on which the *Leonora* had met her fate. Hayes had brought no one with him, and when, after sailing half-way across, he found the wind failing, and a strong ebb setting him sea-ward, he uttered an exclamation of anger at his folly in coming alone, and took to the oars, for in another half hour it would be dark.

From where they stood in front of the deserted house the supercargo and Hope watched him, pulling vigorously, but keep-ing, as they saw to their alarm, dangerously close to the reef, and passing between several outlying boulders of coral rock on which every now and then the swell broke heavily. But they saw him twice lift the foot of the mainsail, look round ahead and then alter his course.

He was just rounding the horn of the reef, when suddenly a flash of white gleamed in the blue water, and the oar in his right hand was torn from his grasp by a shark. Almost at the same moment a sea lifted the boat and dropped her with a crash right on the top of a small coral boulder. She would soon have stove had not the next sea turned her completely over.

The supercargo went sick with fear. He knew what had happpened to half a dozen of those on the *Leonora*, when they were struggling in the water on the night of the wreck almost at the same spot—the place was literally infested with sharks, not of a great size, but particularly daring and ferocious. Time after time since that he had seen oars torn away from boats and paddles from the hands of natives in canoes.

Seizing his gun he fired a shot in the hope that the sound would be heard at Hayes's village, and a boat be sent to his rescue. Then he lifted up the canoe, and carried it to the water, as Hope, who was frantic with fear, now gave a cry of joy, and called out that the captain had come up, and was getting on the top of the boat, which was floating bottom upwards, and being carried on towards them by the swell.

"The paddle, Hope! the paddle! Where is the paddle?" he cried to the boy, as he ran back to the house to search for it. It could not be found.

"Quick, look among the bushes, and about the beach for it," he shouted, as he began to extemporise one from the dead branch of a coconut tree, by cutting off three or four feet of the thin end, and slicing away the leaves. "If you can't find it, I will make this do."

He finished his task, and began to run down to the beach again—when he stopped in mingled anger and amazement. Hope was in the canoe paddling vigorously away from the shore!

"Come back, Hope! Come back!" he shouted. "*You* cannot help the captain; come back, come back."

The boy turned his head for a moment.

"The canoe is too small for thee, Tuhi. We should perish together."

"And you will perish alone, foolish boy!" cried the man in desperation. "Come back, or"—he picked up and levelled his gun—"I shall fire and hurt thee."

Hope knew it was an empty threat, but bent low over his paddle as he struck it quickly into the water again and again, and sent the canoe swiftly along. "Do not shoot at me, Tuhi," he cried out pantingly. "Let me go. Thou wouldst sink the canoe with thy weight. And if the captain be eaten by the sharks, then shall I perish with him!"

The supercargo flung down his gun despairingly on the sand, and then tried one last resource.

"Go on then, you little fool," he shouted in English; "go on and be capsized, and eaten by the sharks. I will swim," and stripping off his clothes, he ran into the water, and began swimming swiftly after the canoe, hoping that the boy would not persist in his intention of going off alone.

Hope turned on his seat and half-rose, and the tears streamed down his brown cheeks.

"Tuhi, dear Tuhi, turn back," he sobbed pitifully; "do not follow. The sharks are many, and they will see thy white skin far off. Turn back, dear Tuhi, turn back to the shore."

The supercargo did not answer. He was looking ahead at Hayes, whose voice could now be heard·shouting to them both.

"Go back, man! Go back, for God's sake!" he cried. "Do you want to be turned into shark's meat? And you too, Hope, go back. If you come a yard further, I'll half-kill you when I get ashore, you young villain."

He was seated astride the keel with his legs drawn up out of the water, and paddling with one of the bottom boards;

which had floated up; and aided by the
inshore counter current, he was slowly
but surely drawing near to shallow water.
But swimming round and round the boat,
biting and tearing at her submerged sails,
and lashing the water into foam as they
tugged fiercely at the thin, tough drill,
were four or five sharks. Sometimes one
of them would make a rush at the boat,
attracted by Hayes' feet, and slide its
huge grey head and shoulders half way
up to the boat's keel.

"Go back! go back!" thundered Hayes to
the supercargo. "I'm all right. Go back,
for God's sake, or they'll see you in another
minute or two. Hope, you damned young
devil, I'll shake the life out of you if you
don't hurry on."

Hope stood up, and looked first at the
captain on the boat, then at his friend
Tuhi, who was now swimming as hard as he
could for the shore—for what mortal man
is there, except those of some native races,

that has not a deadly terror of a shark under such circumstances, and this man had seen some dreadful sights, and heard many dying screams the night the *Leonora* was lost.

"Get ashore at once, you little fool," he cried angrily to the boy; "what are you standing up for like that? Sit down and paddle. Do you want the sharks to see you, you little beast?"

Hope looked round him again—irresolutely. The canoe was midway between the boat and the swimming man. Suddenly he stooped, plunged his paddle rapidly into the water for twenty or thirty strokes, and shot up to within as many yards of the supercargo. Then he slipped quietly overboard, and began swimming vigorously after the white man.

"You little idiot!" gasped the supercargo in angry astonishment, as he turned his head, "what the deuce did you jump overboard for?"

15

"Never mind me, Tuhi," was the brave little fellow's answer. "I am a quick swimmer, and will soon catch thee up. Nay, turn not back; for then shall I turn back and swim to the boat. I swear it. *I shall. I shall.*"

The boy indeed was a noble swimmer, for he came of a race of swimmers. Yet every now and then he kept turning his head, and watching the progress of the captain, though still calling out to the supercargo—

"Go on, Tuhi, go on. I am coming; I am coming."

In a few minutes the white man gained the edge of the inner reef fringing the beach, and stood up. Hope was not far behind. As soon as he was within a few feet of where the supercargo was standing, the latter exploded in wrath, for the boy was smiling.

"You young devil. What the blazes are you grinning at ?"

"Nothing, Tuhi," he replied meekly, as his shapely brown hand clutched the coral ledge, and drawing himself up out of the water, he stood beside his friend.

As soon as Hayes brought the boat into shallow water, they righted her, then went ashore to wait for another boat from Utwe.

.   .   .   .   .   .

"What made you run away from Tuhi?" said Hayes, bending his deep set eyes sternly on the boy.

"Capitan, be not vexed. I found not one, but two paddles lying under a bush. And I knew that if Tuhi went in the canoe it would fill, and the sharks would eat him. But I am but small and light, and I did want to get to thee on the boat with the two paddles, one for thee, and one for me."

"Ah, I see," said Hayes softly, and he placed his hand gently on Hope's shoulder; "that was a good thought, boy. But what made you jump overboard from the canoe?"

Hope bent his eyes to the ground, and made no answer.

"Answer," said Hayes, sharply.

"Because——" and then the childish treble died away.

"Because what?" said Hayes, bending down.

"Because," he whispered, "I was between Tuhi and the sharks . . . and his skin is white . . . and the sharks can see far. . . . And they would have come to me first."

Hayes lifted him off his feet and pressed him to his broad chest. And the supercargo saw that 'Bully's' eyes were filled with tears.

COLLISON'S
TREASURE TROVE

CHAPTER I.

ONE Collison, a trader, was looking lazily
out upon the sea from his store window,
smoking his pipe of strong black 'Barratt's
Twist' tobacco, and wondering what he
should do to pass the day, when a woman
came up the rocky, winding path from the
village, and said, "*Talofa, Pita, ke malolo
koe?*"[1]

"I am well, mother," he replied good-
naturedly, glancing carelessly at the
woman (who was a stranger to him) and
noting that she was old and toil-worn by

[1] Good-day, Peter; are you well?

continuous labour in the taro patches and yam plantations. The remains of a print *teputa*, or bodice, hung loosely from her wrinkled neck, and partly concealed the upper portion of her figure, and around her waist were many folds of tappa, as old and ragged as the bodice. She was evidently some poor widow or dependant, and had, he thought, no doubt come to beg. And presently, as if to confirm him in his opinion, she looked up timidly and said hesitatingly—

"Pita."

"Aye, mother. What wouldst thou?"

"I am Monoa, and a stranger to thee, for I live on the *itu pāpā* (ironbound coast) and thou hast never before seen me. But thou hast been kind to my son."

"Who is thy son, good mother?" said the trader.

"Marengo Lima-tasi.[1] And now he is sick and like to die, and I am old and poor,

[1] Marengo, the One-handed.

and come to thee. Wilt give me *vailaakau* (medicine) for my son ?"

"Aye, willingly," replied the trader sympathisingly, "for Marengo hath been a good son to thee, and 'tis hard that he hath not two hands wherewith to work as other men, for he is strong and of good heart."

The old woman smiled, well pleased, and then Collison asked her to describe the nature of her son's illness, and was soon satisfied that the man had taken a very severe cold which had settled on his chest.

Bidding her come inside into the sitting-room, he bade his cook give her some food, for the poor old creature was not only hungry, but tired out as well with a long walk of many miles along the stern, iron-bound coast. She seated herself cross-legged on the floor and waited patiently while he took out the necessary remedies from his stock of medicines.

"Linseed meal with a good dash of mustard is the thing, I reckon," he said to

himself, as he looked for an empty tin.
Then he bethought himself that simple as
was the remedy it would need to be properly
applied. So he came to the door and
said—

"See, mother. Here is *vailaakau* which
will take away the bad pains and the noisy
breathing in Marengo's chest. But 'tis
better I went with thee, so that I may mix
the medicines together."

"Thou art kind indeed, good friend, to
me—who am stricken with poverty. But
my son and I will repay thee when the
guavas be ripe."

Collison laughed. "Trouble not about
payment for the medicine, Monoa. Am I
a miser that I should hoard up that which
is of no value to me when I am well and
strong? But yet a basket of guavas will I
take from thee—as goodwill to me. Now,
eat. And when thou hast eaten we shall go ;
'tis more to my mind to walk with thee along
the cliffs to Fatiausala and see thy sick son

than to idle away the day here in my house. For to-day is but as one of many when I neither sell nor buy, for until the coconuts are well ripened I have naught to pass the time but my gun and my fishing line;" and then he sighed to himself, for there was indeed but little trading to do at that time of the year, and he was a poor man, fretting at enforced idleness.

Old Monoa finished her meal in silence. Then the trader gave her a cigarette, and lighting his pipe again, told his one servant to bring his gun and shooting bag, as he was ready to start.

"Stay but a little, Pita," and Monoa took out from the folds of her tappa waist-cloth a small round packet, or rather bundle, tied up in the dried frond-leaf of a cabbage palm.

"See," she said, rising to her feet and coming over to him. "We—my son and I—are very, very poor. We have but little land and none of our blood are left to help

us when hunger comes; and I am old, and
he hath but the one hand, and but for thee
he would have *toa'i* (committed suicide), for
he is a proud man. But thou hast given
him work to do — work easy to his one
hand, and so he and I have lived, and
begged from no one. But this morning he
said to me, as he gave me this thing of
apa (metal): 'Take this to the white man,
and tell him I am sick, and yet will not
beg. But this piece of metal may please
his eye, and he will give me medicine for
it.'"

She handed the packet to Còllison. He
unfastened the leaf, and took out a small
but heavy silver flagon, richly chased, and
lined with gold. It was greatly dented,
and showed signs of much usage, but Col-
linson, who had seen such things before in
the life he had now almost forgotten, recognised its antique workmanship, and knew
its value.

"'Tis made of *tupe sina*" (silver), he said,

- "and worth many dollars—more than such a poor man as I can give. So take it back. I want nothing from thee for the little I do."

"Then it is thine—my son sends it as a gift."

"Nay, I cannot take it. When a ship comes let Marengo offer it to the captain for a money price, or for such other things as he may want. It is worth many dollars. How many I cannot tell—twenty, thirty, a hundred—I know not."

For some minutes the old woman urged him to take the gift, and he as steadfastly refused, though tempted to buy it. Then only when she threatened to cast it over the cliffs into the sea, did he provisionally accept it.

"Whence came this cup?" he asked, as he put it in a drawer, which he locked. "'Twas made a full hundred years since."

"I cannot tell thee," she said in a low voice.

Collison asked her no further questions
on the matter, and a few minutes later he
stepped out of the house, gun on shoulder,
followed by the old woman. Passing
through the outskirts of the sleepy village,
they took a path that led them first through
the forest, and then out towards the sea
shore, where the rest of their way lay along
the beetling, rugged cliffs for many miles.

For two hours they followed the narrow,
tortuous tract, which in some places traversed level ground covered with a dense
low scrub, so closely matted overhead with
thorny vines and tangled creepers that the
white man had to stoop; at others it
abruptly descended the side of some deep
canyon, crossed it, and again ascended to
the summits of the grey, stern cliffs, which,
on that part of the lonely sterile coast,
started sheer upwards from the boiling surf,
seven hundred feet below. No sign of
human occupancy relieved the weary eye,
for the land between the sea and the

mountains was, for the most part, stony,
scrub-covered, and barren of aught but the
poorest vegetation, and not even the cry of
a wood pigeon disturbed its forbidding
solitude by day, though the holes and
crannies in the stark wall of stone that
faced the ocean re-echoed with the
clamorous notes of countless thousands of
sea-birds which rested there at night.

"Come, mother, let us rest awhile," said
Collison to old Monoa as they emerged upon
an open sward, covered with coarse saline
grass, and felt the strong blast of the trade
wind in their heated faces. He could see
that she was very tired, and he himself was
glad to sit down awhile and enjoy a pipe.
Near to, and growing almost on the brink
of the cliff were a few pandanus palms,
their long, sharp pinnated leaves streaming
pennon-like to the wind and exposing to
view great, heavy green and orange coloured
fruit. Beneath was the blue sea flecked
white with sea-horses, and dashing its

thunderous rollers against the base of the cliffs; above a cloudless sky and a sun of brass, and seemingly near to, but yet far away, the cool, sweet green of the quiet mountain forest.

Collison stretched himself out upon the grass with his soft Panama hat for a pillow; the old woman rolled herself a cigarette in a strip of dried banana leaf, lit it from the white man's pipe, and then in a gentle, timid way, sat down, removed his boots, and began to *mili mili* (or massage) his feet. In a few minutes he sighed contentedly and fell asleep.

.   .   .   .   .   .

Collision was a type of an island trader now all but extinct, except in those out-of-way groups or isolated islands of the north-western Pacific, whether they have been driven for an existence by the advent of the 'storekeeper' pure and simple—the combined grocer and linendraper who displays his wares to European-clad natives over a polished counter like any other grocer or draper in London or New York. For many years he had cruised through the Pacific, first as mate, then as master, till, wearied of the sea, he had begun the usual life of a trader, wandering from group to group and from island to island, making money one year, losing it the next, and yet, while never too hopeful of acquiring a fortune, never despondent, nor wishing to abandon the lonely existence he led and return either to civilisation or to a seafaring life again. Naturally of a cheerful disposition, even under the most adverse circumstances, he also had the great secret of adaptability to his surroundings; and, wherever he settled, he soon gained the respect of the natives by a consistent course of conduct, his untiring energy, his studious observance of the practice never to offend their susceptibilities, and lastly the proficiency with which he spoke half a dozen of the native languages.

He was now fifty years of age, making a fairly good living, though hampered by want of a little capital to extend his trading operations. When he came to Satupaitea— nearly twelve months previous to the opening of this story—he quickly made himself a favourite with the people, and had at first some considerable difficulty in convincing them that he had no need of a wife. He had lived so long alone, he said, with a smile, that he would remain a bachelor till the end.

One day, soon after he had established himself in a village, a sturdy, square-built native about forty years of age, and dressed in a seaman's jumper and pants, came to his store and bought a little tobacco, paying for it with a fresh-water fish. As Collison handed him the tobacco, he saw that the man had lost his left hand. In a sympathetic manner he asked him the cause of such a misfortune, and learnt that it was the result of an accident—a bomb had exploded prematurely when it was being fired at a whale.

"My name," said his visitor, "is Alo, and I belong to Fatiausala, where my mother lives, but everyone calls me 'Marengo.' I sailed in the ship *Marengo* as boatsteerer for two years, and it was when I was firing a bomb from one of her boats off Sunday Island that I lost my hand. That was six years ago. So I came home to live with my mother."

There was something about the man that attracted the trader, who from that day did all that lay in his power to help him. Although so crippled, he was an active, vigorous fellow, eager to work, and Collison found him useful in many ways. If, for instance, the trader had occasion to pay a visit to any of the villages on the coast, he would frequently leave Marengo in charge of his house, paying him not only fairly, but generously, for his caretaking.

Several times Collison had told Marengo

16

that he would one day pay a visit to Fatiausala, a village which he had not yet seen.
But he noticed that the poor fellow did not
express any pleasure, and soon learnt the
reason—he was ashamed of his own and his
mother's poverty, and one day frankly said
so.

"It would grieve my mother, Pita, to
have thee come to our house. We should
have to *fa'aoleole* (beg) to our neighbours
for food to offer thee. And that would
shame us."

Collison understood his feelings, and so
never went to Fatiausala.

CHAPTER II

" BETTER, Marengo ? "

" *Aue* ! I feel strong. My heart has come back to me and I know I shall not die. May I smoke ? "

" No—not for two or three days unless you want to die."

" Then at least let my mother sit near me and blow the smoke from her *sului* (cigarette) into my nostrils."

" Thou little baby," said Collison laughingly, now speaking in Samoan, in which tongue Marengo usually addressed him ; " art not satisfied to wait till thy chest is better ? Perhaps by to-night I may let thee smoke one *sului.*"

Nearly two days had passed since the trader had entered old Monoa's hut at Fatiausala, to find Marengo stretched out upon his sleeping mat, gasping for breath. So serious was his condition that Collison, who knew well how very quickly some Polynesians sink under chest complaints, even of a temporary nature, had very grave doubts of his recovery. But simple as were the remedies applied, they were efficacious, the confidence of the patient in his doctor being no doubt a primary factor towards a rapid recovery. And the man was deeply grateful. Only once had Collison left him, and then but for a few hours, to return to Satupaitea for some tins of soup and other food, which he knew would be better suited for Marengo than the usual indigestible native diet.

The village of Fatiausala consisted of less than a score of houses, and was situated on a small, fertile plateau between two streams, which swept swiftly down from the main range traversing the island, and poured into the sea over the cliffs. The people were very poor, for their joint coconut groves were but of limited extent, and consequently they had no copra (dried coconut) to sell the trading vessels that occasionally passed within hail of the village. The men were all noted fishermen and hunters, and sea and forest gave them, at most times, all the food they needed. In the mountains wild pigs and pigeons were plentiful; the two streams teemed with a species of trout, and when the sea was smooth enough to launch their canoes, they returned laden to the gun-wales with bonito amd other deep water fish.

Within half a mile of the village there was a strip of country of the roughest and wildest description. In ages past some great seismic convulsion had torn away a spur of the mountain range, and hurled it towards the sea, forming hills and valleys, which, as time went on, gradually became so covered with vegetation of a minor character—low, dense scrub, tangled jungle and undergrowth— that it concealed, and gave a certain pleasant aspect of greenness to what was in reality one of the most difficult and dangerous portions of the whole of the iron-bound coast. Even the Fatiausala people avoided the locality, although its border actually touched the confines of the village; for not alone were there deep chasms concealed by a thick overgrowth of vines and creepers into which in years gone by more than one unwary boar hunter had fallen and been killed, but the place was believed to be peopled with evil and cannibal spirits, ever on the watch to seize upon and devour the unfortunate human being who was so reckless or so ignorant as to enter their haunt.

During his attendance on his one-handed

patient, Collison had visited the Ana-o-aitu
(the Caves of the Devils), as the locality
was termed, and returned with a number
of pigeons and wood-doves which he had
shot there—much to the horror of the
villagers, who, with dread depicted on their
countenances, earnestly begged him to at
once destroy the birds by fire, else the
revengeful demons in the caves would
exact some dreadful retribution which
would involve not only himself, but the
whole of Fatiausala in destruction. Without the slightest hesitation he yielded to
their importunities. A fire was lit, the
birds hurriedly burnt, and the villagers
uttered expressions of thankfulness that
all traces of them were destroyed. But
he nevertheless determined to again visit
Ana-o-aitu before he left for his own home,
and try to explore some of the many dark
and mysterious caves and passages, especially
one which was famous in Samoan history
as the scene of a terrible massacre of some

hundreds of people by the ferocious Tama-fiaga, a noted despot of the olden time.

So on the afternoon of the second day, whilst old Monoa was absent, he broached the subject to Marengo, feeling almost sure that he, from his long association with white men, was comparatively free from the superstition that pervaded the rest of the small community of Fatiausala, and would, if he could, tell him the easiest way of penetrating the Ana-o-aitu. He was not mistaken; for Marengo, whilst admitting that he would not dare to go there alone, expressed his willingness to accompany Collison, but said that not even his mother should know of their intention, for she would be terrified, and the rest of the villagers resentful as well, of a proceeding that to their minds would bring some dreadful calamity upon them.

" Very well," said the trader; " we can pretend we are going fishing up the river."

Marengo nodded, and then speaking in English he said suddenly—

"Do you know where that silver *ipu* (jug) came from?"

"No. Do you?"

"Yes. It came from the Ana-o-Aitu. I picked it up there on the day I became sick. My mother was frightened and told me to throw it away, but I would not. And I believe that she thought that I was going to die just because I picked it up; but now that I am better she is not so frightened."

"Where did you find it?"

"In the old stone wall that goes round my mother's yam plantation; there was a part which had fallen down, and while I was mending it with some big stones I found the cup. It was in a hole in the wall, and was covered with moss."

"I wonder who put it there?"

"My mother knows. And she told me that there are many such things in the Ana-

o-aitu. They were hidden there by white
men when she was a girl. No one else
knows it."

Collision uttered an exclamation of surprise, and pressed Marengo for further
particulars.

"Wait till my mother returns, Pita.
She will tell you all about it, I'm sure."

So eager was Collison to hear the old
woman's story, that he became quite restless
as he impatiently waited her return. At
last she appeared coming up from the shore,
carrying a small basketful of *manini*—the
most delicious of all Samoan rock-fish, which
were to be cooked for the evening meal. As
soon as she had divested herself of her wet
fishing garments for a dry *lava-lava* of tappa
cloth, and rolled and lighted the inevitable
cigarette, the trader began to question her
about the Ana-o-Aitu.

At first she was somewhat disconcerted,
and chid her son for telling the white man
—kind as he had been to them—that which

was told to him in confidence. But she could not long withstand Collison's entreaties, especially after Marengo had reproachfully told her that it would be churlish and ungracious of her to refuse such a simple request.

"I will tell thee all, Pita," she said, "and if thou wilt come with me a little way beyond the point to the west, I will show thee the place where the ship was wrecked —the ship from which were taken the things that lie in the Ana-o-aitu. 'Tis but a little distance, and I would not that my neighbours should hear me speaking of the Ana-o-aitu; it would anger them."

Accompanied by Marengo, they left the house and took a well-worn and shady path which led to the village plantations; then passing these, Monoa turned to the west through a thick guava scrub, and in less than a quarter of an hour they found themselves on the point she had mentioned. It was one of the headlands of a very small bay—one of the few indentations on the long line of rocky coast—which was fairly sheltered from the prevailing trade-winds, and was fringed by a narrow strip of beach, through the centre of which debouched a tiny stream. A dense thorny scrub grew close to the water's edge, but further back there were a few scattered coco-palms and screw pines, which relieved the otherwise monotonous aspect of the place. Pointing to the little stream flowing through the beach, Monoa told Collison that although the scrub through which it made its way from the mountains was impenetrable, it could be followed up to within a few hundred yards of the Ana-o-aitu, as, though the bed was rocky, the water was very shallow and very clear. Then she began her story.

"I do not know how many years ago it is since the ship was *tu'ia* (wrecked), but I was quite young and had just married my first husband, who was a man of Falealupo "

(the most westerly settlement of the Samoan
Islands). "And I remember having seen,
when I was a little child, the three ships of
the *Alii sauā Amelika*[1] sailing down the
straits between Savai'i and Upolu.

"My husband came to live with me here
on the *itu pāpā*. Fatiausala was then a
town of nearly a hundred houses, and the
chief Mauafa was known all over Samoa as
a great sorcerer, who could get Mafuie, the
earthquake god, to throw down mountains
and crush villages and turn aside rivers
from their courses. So he was much feared,
and became very rich with the offerings
sent to him from people even as far away
as Tutuila and Manua—sixty leagues away.
But he was very good to his people and did
not oppress them as do some chiefs, and he
made my husband welcome because he (my

[1] Commodore Wilkes of the American Exploring
Expedition which visited Samoa in 1836 was known
as *Le Alii Sauā* (The Cruel Captain) on account of
the severe discipline he maintained in his fleet.

husband) was a very clever maker of bonito canoes, and to be that is, as thou knowest, a great honour in this country.

"One morning, not many months after my marriage, and when the wind was blowing strongly from the westward, we were astonished to see a ship with three masts coming swiftly in towards the land. It had but two sails set, and the upper part of the masts were broken off short. There were a great many men on board, and we could see them running to and fro on the deck in great confusion, and getting ready the anchors. Where we are now sitting, the people of Fatiausala gathered together. I was here with my husband, and Mauafa the chief sat beside us; his eyes were shining with joy, for he knew that the ship would soon become a wreck, and he would get much plunder.

"'They are fools,'" he cried, 'to cast anchor in such a place, for the bottom is rocky and the cables will soon be broken!'

" But all went well with the ship at first, for soon after she anchored, the wind came further from the northward, and the sea grew smoother. Then Mauafa and some of his young men put out in canoes and went on board. The captain made them welcome, and said his ship had been driven on to the land by the loss of many sails. There were more than one hundred men on board, and but two or three could speak English—the rest spoke a language that none of us understood, though two of Mauafa's young men could speak a little English. There were twenty cannons on the ship—ten on each side—and we were told afterwards that she was a *vaa gaoi*,[1] and had come to these seas to seek out and destroy ships of any nation but that of France."

[1] A pirate, or privateer.

CHAPTER III

"The captain took Mauafa into the cabin,
and gave him wine to drink, and biscuits to
eat, and said he wanted to buy fresh provisions, and fill the ship's water casks.
Mauafa promised him fish and fowls, and
said there was good water running into the
bay. As they talked, three white ladies
came in and looked at them; the captain
made Mauafa understand that these women
were the wives of himself and two of his
officers. They were all very young, and at
first seemed frightened at our people, but
their fear soon wore off.

"Towards noon the sea was so calm that
two boats from the ship were lowered, and

256

'The Captain rushed back to his boat, when one of his own crew drew his pis
and shot him through the chest."

[*See page*

sent on shore to the river's mouth with
water casks; our people helped to fill them.
All the white men were armed—each had
two pistols and a sword, and in each boat
there were many muskets as well. Presently the captain himself came ashore with
his wife, and scarcely had he placed his foot
on the beach when there arose the sound of
a great commotion on the ship, and firing
of guns. The captain rushed back to his
boat, when one of his own crew drew his
pistol and shot him through the chest. He
fell into the water, and then some other
men from all three boats ran up and hacked
at him with their swords. But there were
some few who tried to save him, and these
began shooting at those who had killed him.
But they were too few in number, and the
others soon slew them all and threw their
bodies into the sea.

"Whilst this was being done, the woman
sat quite quiet in the boat and watched
them. Some of our people said that when

17

she saw the captain fall, she was pleased
and clapped her hands and laughed. All
this time there was continual firing going
on on board the ship, and when it ceased,
we saw dead and wounded men being thrown
overboard. Some who were not badly hurt
tried to get on board again, but those on
deck shot them or killed them with swords.

"There were on the ship at this time
several of our people—women—who saw all
the fighting. They were in the cabin with
the two other white ladies, when suddenly
a sailor entered with a drawn sword and
stood at the door. He said something to the
white women, who were much frightened,
but he did them no harm. Then began
shooting on deck, and a great din of cries
and stamping. When it was all over, there
came into the cabin four men—all *awaa*
(common seamen). Their swords were
dripping with blood, and one who was the
leader called to the white women for wine.
The four men were soon followed by many

more, some of whom were wounded, till
the cabin was full of them, and then the
leader put his cap on the point of his sword
and held it on high, and the rest of the
men shouted together, and then they all
laughed and drank wine in plenty; and
whilst they were drinking, the captain's
wife came in with the men who had killed
her husband. She ran up to the leader,
and threw her arms around him and kissed
him, and held a cup of wine for him to
drink. He was quite a young man with
black curly hair, and had gold rings in his
ears.

"Finding that no harm was meant to any
of our people, Mauafa and a man named
Sali, who could speak English, came on
board. The young man shook the chief's
hand, and told Sali that he was now captain
and that all the officers but the gunner and
the *fo'mai* (doctor) had been killed. He
gave Mauafa some good presents—a musket
and a sword and two axes, and promised

him more when the water casks were filled,
and the ship ready to sail. Then all the
men sat down together, and the new captain
talked to them. The old captain's wife sat
by his side, the two other women next to
her.

"Presently he ceased, and then the *fo'mai*
rose and came over and sat beside the
woman who had been wife to one of the
officers. She wept, but all the men shouted
and seemed pleased. Then the captain
spoke again, looking at the third woman,
who was very fair, and had yellow hair.
As he spoke, two men stood up, and the
captain pointed to them both. She bent
her head and would not look up, though
the woman seated next to the captain tried
hard to make her raise her head.

"Suddenly the captain struck his hand
angrily on the table, and called for everyone
to follow him on deck. Here he bade the
two men, each of whom claimed the yellow-
haired woman, to fight. They did so, and

in a little time the older of the two struck
his sword into the other man's throat. He
fell, and died very quickly.

"All that day and night there was re-
joicing on board the ship, and nearly all
the white men became very drunk, and lay
about the decks like wallowing hogs.
Some, however, were sober, and they and
the new captain urged Mauafa to hasten
with the work of filling the water casks.
By nightfall this was nearly done.

"Now Mauafa was disappointed that the
wind had died away, for he had hoped that
it would continue to blow, so that the ship's
cable, which was not iron, but rope, would
be chafed through by the sharp coral, and
the ship be driven on shore. So that
night he and Sali and some others plotted
to swim off and cut it. And this would
have been accomplished were it not that
other things befel; for at midnight there
began fresh quarrelling on the ship, and
we heard three or four guns fired and the

clash of arms. Many of us ran to the
shore, or to where we now sit, and watched.
The moon was very bright, and we saw
the figures of two men lying on the after
deck, surrounded by the new captain and
many men. Then we heard a scream, and
the woman with the yellow hair rushed
up from the cabin and cast herself overboard. In an instant the ship was in an
uproar, and some of the men jumped into
one of the boats, and sought to save the
women; but she had sunk quickly. The
men in the boat pulled round and round
the ship many times and then searched no
longer. Scarcely had they returned when
there came a great outcry, and we saw a
thick cloud of smoke arise out of the fore
part where the sailors live; flame soon
followed, and then a number of men rushed
towards the stern. The clothing of some
of them was on fire, and in an instant there
was great terror and confusion. So many
of the men were in a drunken sleep that

those who were sober could do little to save
the ship, for now the flames were shooting
up high, and presently some one cut the
cable and others hoisted some of the head
sails, so that the ship's bow fell away from
the wind, and in a little time she began to
move on towards the shore. She struck
the ground when about a hundred fathoms
from the beach, and then the boats were
brought to the side, and the sailors began
to load them with many things. Many of
our canoes went to help, and in the first
boat that came ashore were the two
women.

" All this time the fire in the belly of
the ship was burning fiercely, though the
captain had had many holes made in her
side, so that the water might flow in.
There were three boats, and each of these
came several times to the shore laden with
many things, which were cast out upon the
beach, where they were guarded by a few
men. It took them a long time before the

last boatload was brought on shore, and by that time the fire in the underneath part of the ship had gone out, for she was filled with water; but had it not been for the rising tide, all that part of her above water would have been consumed.

"When the morning came, the captain went off to look at the ship and brought some more things away. Then he told Mauafa that she was now worthless to him and his men, so our people flocked off on board and took whatever was left, but they were not given much time, for before it was noon-day a heavy sea began to rush into the bay, and the vessel to break up. In two days there was naught left to be seen but the broken wood cast high up on the beach. All the twenty cannons were lost, and most of them lie buried where the ship struck; four only did Mauafa save long after, and used them in his wars, with round stones for shot.

"The white men made a rough sort of

fort — for they did not trust our people, though we had given no cause for suspicion. At the end of five days they began to prepare the three boats, and then they made a division of all things they had brought on shore. There was much money—gold and silver, and hundreds and hundreds of muskets and steel spears, and kegs of powder and bullets, and *itula* (clocks and watches) and swords and daggers. All this was divided into three lots. Then there was left a pile of things we had never seen before, among which were hundreds and hundreds of silver cups and plates, and lamps. These they put into bags of canvas, boxes and small barrels, and then, to our astonishment, they one day carried them up the stream towards the Ana-o-aitu, though we had told them that it was a place of horror, and meant death to anyone who put foot there. Before they began to do this, the captain called Sali to him and said, 'Tell your chief that I want him and some of his people to help me to carry all these things to the broken country,' pointing to the Ana-o-aitu, 'where I shall hide them till I return here in another ship. And tell him that these things are of no value to him, and so I trust him to keep secret from any white men the spot where they are placed. For reward I shall now give him four muskets, a keg of bullets, one of powder, and ten pieces of rich silk, each twenty fathoms in length.'

"This Sali told the chief, who answered quickly—

"'If thou didst offer me all that thou hast—all thy guns and swords, and powder, and all else that thou hast saved from the ship—neither I nor any man of mine would go with thee to the Ana-o-aitu. And this more do I tell thee—if thou or any one of thy people doth but put foot in that place, thou wilt perish miserably, and so be warned.'

"The captain did not seem angry at

Mauafa's words, neither did his men; but each one taking up a burden they boldly set out, the captain leading, for he had been told that by following the little river up stream he would come to the caves. We watched them go with fear and horror, and great was our astonishment when they returned safely.

"That evening the captain gave Mauafa many presents, especially axes, knives, rope, cordage, and bales and bundles of white and coloured cloth. Then when the morning came, the three boats were manned, and he and the two women bade us farewell. Each boat was filled with men, all of whom took arms with them. Before he left he asked us which was the best place to look for *vaa so'ia* (whale-ships), and we told him that if he went to the eastward through the straits to Apia or Falifa in Upolu, that there would he find perhaps three or four, if he hastened, for now was the time when they sailed northward from Samoa for the islands of the Tokleau.

He was pleased, and said if all went well with him we should see him back with another ship ere a month was gone.

"But no one of them ever returned, and we heard many months afterwards that they all perished one night on the reef between Manono and Mulifanua, for pieces of the boats were washed ashore, and guns and other things were found in the pools on the reef.

"Long, long years passed, during which time we never saw another white man. Mauafa was ever at war with his neighbours, and in his pride attacked Palaulae. He was beaten off, and then we suffered, for Palaulae made alliance with Manono, and in one day Fatiausala was given to the flames, and every one but a few women and children slaughtered. My husband was among the slain, but I was taken to Manono and given in marriage to the father of Marengo."

She ceased, and Collison, now greatly excited, though he did not show it, asked her if no white man but himself had ever heard of the story of the things hidden in the Ana-o-aitu?

She shook her head. " None—none. For from the very day the things had been taken there we lived in dread. Mauafa (who was a strong wizard) for many months placed baskets of food at the boundary of the spirits' land to propitiate them for the violation of their abode. And he himself bade us never to speak of what the white men had hidden there."

Collison had heard enough, and that night, when the old woman was fast asleep, he touched Marengo with his foot, and beckoned to him to come outside.

The two talked earnestly together for about a quarter of an hour, and then returned to sleep till daylight.

CHAPTER IV.

AT sunrise, after eating a hurried meal, Collison and Marengo left old Monoa's house, ostensibly on a fishing and shooting expedition; the former carrying his gun and game bag, and the latter a bamboo fishing rod. Fearful of being followed by some of the few children of the village, who would be eager to accompany them, they got past the houses as quickly as possible, and made direct for Monoa's plantation, which, as has been mentioned, was almost on the verge of the Ana-o-aitu.

As soon as they reached the low stone wall which enclosed the plantation, Marengo showed the trader the spot where he had

found the cup. How it came to be hidden
in such a spot was, Collison thought, easily
explainable, for although the wall itself was
quite two hundred yards away from the
beginning of the series of caverns and clefts,
it was very much lower down, and the cup
had probably been dropped by accident, and
then subsequently found after the rest of
the articles had been hidden, and the finder
had thrust it into a hole in the wall, which
even in those days was an old structure,
mossgrown and bound together with vines
and a species of thin, thorny cane.

Outside the wall, the two men paused to
consider whether they should ascend or
descend, for far below them they could hear
the little stream which debouched into the
bay coursing over its rocky bed, and
Marengo thought it would be easier to get
into the heart of the Ana-o-aitu by keeping
to the stream than by forcing a way up and
down through the tangled undergrowth,
and climbing over the huge boulders of

stone which would everywhere bar their
progress. So it was decided to make for
the stream.

The early morn was very calm and
beautiful; the soft murmur of the mountain
stream was answered a mile away by the
measured beat of the surf on the rocky
coast, and from every tree around came the
soft plaintive coo of wood doves (the
manutagi or 'crying-bird' of the Samoans),
the deep boom of the blue pigeon, and the
shrill chatter of the *fuia*, a bird of jet black
plumage, as large as a thrush. Far above,
the tops of the green clad mountains were
yet veiled in a thin grey mist, and to the
westward was the sea, waiting for the first
breath of trade wind to ruffle its placid
bosom.

"Come," said Marengo, "let us go."

He led the way down, and crippled as
he was, the trader found it difficult to keep
up with him. In a few minutes they
were at the bottom and standing beside the

stream, which at this spot was about ten yards across from bank to bank, which were thickly lined with trees, the branches almost meeting overhead, and obscuring the sunlight. The bed of the stream was formed of loose stones, but the water was so very clear that they had no trouble in keeping their footing.

Suddenly there came a sharp turn to the right, the light became stronger, the timber more open, and huge boulders of stone appeared scattered about, both on the banks and in the water. Stepping out on to the bank they now followed the course of the stream with ease for nearly a quarter of a mile, when it became lost in a labyrinth of immense jagged rocks piled loosely together in the wildest confusion, and all covered to their bases with a network of dead and living creepers.

For some time they were undecided which way to turn, when suddenly Marengo uttered an exclamation and pointed to the

18

left hand bank, and Collison felt sure that
they had found the spot for which they
sought.

Less than thirty yards away was what
appeared to be a high, irregular and over-
hanging wall, the face of which was for
the most part covered with pendant trailers
of a thorny creeper, and a climbing plant
resembling ivy. Here and there, however,
were large holes or openings, extending
back into the wall for many feet, and in
the largest of these there was plainly
visible from where they stood, piled on
a heap of loose stones, a number of
muskets.

Collison was the first to reach the place,
and step into the cave—if it could so be
called—for the floor of it was not more
than two or three feet from the ground.
It was not more than a dozen feet in
length and eight or ten in width, and
there, tumbled together in confusion,
were barrels, cases, firearms, carpenter's

tools, and a pile of what had once been silks and bolts of canvas, but had now rotted away under the influence of time and the moist, humid atmosphere. Not the slightest attempt had been made at concealment, though that could easily have been accomplished by blocking up the opening with loose stones, and letting Nature do the rest by means of the tangle of moss and creepers which would have soon bound them together and given the opening the same appearance as the greater portion of the natural wall.

Tossing aside the rusting and rotting arms, axes, and the decayed rolls of silk and bolts of canvas, Collison and his companion soon knocked in the head of the first barrel. It was filled to the chine with silver plate, heavy and massive. Nearly everything that Collison examined had engraved upon it the word 'Cècile'— doubtless the name of the unfortunate ship from which it had been plundered, or perhaps that of the privateer herself. A second barrel and two small heavy boxes were filled to the brim with similar articles, some of which bore the crest of the Honourable East India Company, and some, of a totally distinct and more chaste design, the word 'Duyphen.' Thrown carelessly in amongst the services of plate were a number of silver-mounted tops and stoppers of decanters and other glass ware which had been broken off to economise space, silver and gold sword hilts, lace, and other military adornments, and several beautifully made clocks, ivory work-boxes, and delicately carved Indian ornaments inlaid with gold and silver.

It did not take Collison long to decide upon a plan of action, and he at once took Marengo into his confidence. Their discovery, he determined, should remain a secret between them.

"You must help me to get all these

things to my own house, Marengo. It
will take us many days to do it, as we
must only bring away a little at a time.
Now, listen, and I will tell you how we
shall do it."

Half an hour afterwards they set to
work, and by noon half of the treasure
had been carried down the stream to a
spot near the sea, where it would be within
a few minutes' walk from the landing
place.

Then after shooting a few pigeons and
catching some fish, so as not to cause
comment from the villagers by returning
empty - handed, they returned to old
Monoa's house, and after resting a while,
Collison announced his intention of returning to his own place. He made a point,
however, of openly stating to some of the
people that he should probably return in
his boat on his way to the town of
Falealupo, and perhaps stay a night and
part of the next day. With that he dis-

tributed a few presents, bade them *' to fa,'* and went off, highly elated.

As soon as ever he reached home that day he began his preparations by making a rough false bottom over the floor of his boat, by raising the bottom boards ten inches, telling the natives who watched him at work that he meant to make the boat more comfortable for a trip to Falealupo by taking out her iron ballast and substituting sand bags.

With the first streak of daylight he made a start, anxious to get off before any of the people could volunteer to come with him. He had never before sailed off alone on any of his occasional trading trips, but this time he did not want any company. Hoisting the mainsail and jib, he quietly lifted his anchor, and was soon running down the coast. By ten o'clock he had reached the little bay near Fatiausala, anchored his boat at the mouth of the

stream, and, gun in hand, sauntered up
to the village.

After chatting a little while with some
of the people, he asked Marengo to come
shooting with him, and the two started off
in a leisurely manner towards the mountains. Once out of sight of the village
they quickened their pace till they were
in old Monoa's plantation, where Marengo
had in readiness two new and strongly
made baskets of coconut leaf. Taking
these, they descended to the stream, and
were soon at work filling them with the
silver.

Three or four hours later their work was
completed, and every article had been safely
conveyed to the boat. All that could not
be stowed under the false floor they put
into ballast bags, and filled up the interstices
with broken coral debris or sand, without
being seen by a single person.

Then Marengo went back to the village,
and told his mother that the white man

had forgotten to bring a box of tobacco,
intended for trading purposes at Falealupo,
and he (Marengo) was going back in the
boat with him to get it.

Late that night the boat sailed quietly
up to the beach of Collison's village, and in
the darkness the trader and Marengo carried
everything up to the house, and placed it
in safety without attracting attention, for
the dwelling stood alone, and the people
did not even know that the boat had returned.

    •   •   •   •

A month later, Collison made his appearance in Apia, accompanied by old Monoa
and her one-armed son. To the surprise of
his acquaintances, he announced his intention
of going to Australia for a few months, and
said that he hoped to buy a small vessel and
return to the islands before the year was
out.

Before leaving, he acted most generously
to the old woman and her son, by buying

a piece of fertile land in the Vaisigago Valley, and giving them five hundred dollars in cash.

When Collison returned to Samoa, he was owner and master of one of the smartest cutters ever seen in the island trade. He had realised over two thousand pounds by the sale of the silver, and was well content.

Then he sailed westward for the Solomon Islands, convinced that his luck had turned at last, and that he would not die a poor man. Nor was he mistaken, for he is now, if not wealthy, one of the most prosperous of the old-time traders who ever sailed the Southern Seas.

.ve the boat the much-dreaded 'under-clip' with his flukes, and tossed
her high in the air."   (See page 294.)

[*Frontispiece.*

"He gave the boat a most elevated summerset, with his heels high in the air." (See page 204.)

'FIGHTING' WHALES

NOT long ago the writer received a letter from an old friend and a former shipmate (now engaged in the Torres Straits pearl-fishery) in which he referred to a mutual acquaintance, the master of a vessel trading among the islands of the Paumotu group. "Rennett," he wrote, "had a narrow squeak last February in the Paumotus. He was all but becalmed at eight o'clock in the morning, when three or four whales were sighted about three miles away. They were 'breaching' (throwing themselves bodily out of the water), and no notice was taken of them until half an hour later, when one of them was seen to be quite close to the

schooner and coming at her like a bull at a
gate. Before anyone on board thought
about getting rifles on deck, he put on a
spurt and hit the ship on the port bow and
nearly sent her to the bottom, for Rennet
had a task to keep her afloat. Only for a
bit of a breeze coming on he would have
had to have taken to his boats. However,
he managed to get inside the lagoon and
run her ashore on the beach."

There are many notable instances on
record of whales actually charging and
sinking large vessels, either from malice
aforethought when agonised by wounds in-
flicted on them by harpoon and lance, or
from mere playfulness. For huge as is his
bulk the sperm whale has, like the porpoise,
a sense of fun, and at times amuses himself
by 'breaching,' rolling over and over with
opened mouth, and thrashing the sea with
his mighty flukes, indulging in the same
movements as he does when attacked by
sword-fish, 'threshers,' or the dreaded

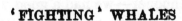

'killers.' These latter creatures are themselves a small species of whale, and their
jaws are armed with short but powerful
teeth; and any reader of this article can
see what they are like by visiting the new
whale room in the South Kensington
Museum, where there are one or two moder-
ately-sized specimens. The 'killer' (*Orca
gladiator*) is, however, such an extra-
ordinary creature that he deserves an
article to himself, so for the present I shall
confine myself to the subject of 'fighting'
whales.

My first experience dates back more than
twenty years ago, in the Friendly Islands
(Tonga). The *Niger* and two other New
Bedford whale-ships, whose names I cannot
now remember, were cruising in company
between the island of Tongatabu and the
Vavau group when at daylight one morning a
number of sperm whales were sighted, and
every ship lowered boats. The wind was
light, and from our own vessel—a small

trading schooner—we had a good view of the
exciting work. In less than half an hour
five boats were 'fast' to as many whales,
others following the remaining 'loose' fish,
which made off to windward, as they invari-
ably do when 'gallied' (frightened). One
of the *Niger* boats was fast to a bull, and
was being hauled up to him to use the
lance, when he 'sounded,' and making a
'mill' or turn hundreds of fathoms below,
suddenly shot upwards and caught the boat
between his jaws, crushing her to pieces;
the crew escaping by a miracle. He then
sounded again, but soon reappeared,
swimming round and round with head well
out of the water, but evidently in trouble
with the line, which had become wound
about his body and flukes. A second boat
belonging to one of the other ships went to
the rescue of the *Niger* men, picked them
up, and at once started for the whale, who
was now making the most violent efforts to
free himself of the line and of the iron

embedded in his body. The boat, greatly
overcrowded by the additional men, pulled
right up to him and a second and then a
third iron plunged into his monstrous frame.
He at once sounded, and then again
'milled,' rose, with a burst of foam, and
made for the boat, with his lower jaw dis-
tended. The officer was an old and ex-
perienced whaleman—a Western Islands
Portuguese—and just succeeded in giving
the boat a sheer sufficient to escape that
cavernous mouth with its appalling teeth,
when up went the mighty flukes, and up, too,
went the boat, and a dozen men were sent
flying in the air.

Our own schooner and the *Niger* at once
each sent a boat to pick up the men, just in
time to save one man from sinking. A
second man, a fine stalwart young Kanaka,
a native of Rotumah Island, was lifted in
in an unconscious state, but soon recovered ;
but a third—the boatsteerer of the first boat
that had struck the whale—came off worst of

all, for he had a broken collar-bone, and a splinter of wood driven into his arm from the elbow right up to the shoulder, from which it protruded.   All these men we took on board the schooner in our boat, while that from the whaleship started off again after the bull, who was now following the loose whales to windward, stopping every now and then and trying to clear himself from the enormous length of line he was towing, some of which was still entangled around his 'small' and flukes.   The boat-header of the fresh boat was a little wizened-up old man with the command of an extensive vocabulary of whaler's 'language,' and his crew sent the beautiful craft along like an arrow shot from a bow.   After a short chase he succeeded in getting near enough to the enraged whale to have fired a bomb into him, but disdaining this, he put another iron into him and soon after-wards he hauled up to and killed him with two or three lance thrusts, for the creature died so quickly that his 'flurry' lasted but a few minutes.

When this whale was being cut-in, there was found buried deep in the blubber on his back a harpoon in a perfect state of preservation, though it had been there for perhaps twenty years. It was of English make, and the officers of the whalers were of the opinion that it had probably belonged to a Sydney or Hobart Town ship on account of its old-fashioned style.

A few years ago there arrived in Sydney Harbour from Kaipara, in New Zealand, a fine barquentine of three hundred tons named the *Handa Isle*, which had fared badly from an encounter with a whale.

The present writer described the incident as follows :—The barquentine was sailing over a smooth sea with a moderate breeze when two whales were sighted. They were travelling very quickly, and suddenly altering their course made for the ship. Then one sounded, but the other continued

19

his furious way and deliberately charged
the barquentine. He struck her with
terrific force amidships and just below the
water-line. Fortunately the *Handa Isle*
was laden with a cargo of timber, otherwise she would have foundered instantly.
The blow was fatal to the cetacean, for
in a few minutes the water around the
ship was seen to be crimsoned with blood,
and presently the mighty creature rose
to the surface again, beat the ensanguined water feebly with his monstrous
tail, and then slowly sunk.

Here is another instance. " A small
'pod' or school of whales were sighted
off Strong Island, one of the · Caroline
Archipelago, by the ship *St George* of
New Bradford and the Hawaiian brig
Kamehameha IV. Both ships lowered
their boats together, and in a very short
time Captain Wicks of the Hawaiian brig
got fast to a very large bull who was
cruising by himself about half a mile away

from the rest of the 'pod.' As is not
uncommon with sperm and humpbacked
whales, the rest of the school, almost the
instant their companion was struck, showed
their consciousness of what had occurred,
and crowded closely together in the
greatest alarm, lying motionless on the
surface of the water as if listening, and
sweeping their huge flukes slowly to and
fro as a cat sweeps its tail when watching
for an expected spring from one of its own
kind. So terrified were they with the
knowledge that some unknown and in-
visible danger beset them that they per-
mitted the 'loose' boats—five in number
—to pull right on top of them. Four of
the boats at once got fast to as many
whales without difficulty, leaving three
or four still huddled together in the
greatest fear and agitation. Just as the
fifth boat got within striking distance of
the largest of the remaining fish, he suddenly sounded, and was immediately.

followed by the others. Some minutes passed before Martin, the officer of the fifth boat, could tell which way they had gone, when the *St George* signalled 'Gone to windward,' and presently Martin saw them running side by side with the whale which had been struck by Captain Wicks. Martin at once started off to intercept them, and when within a few hundred yards he saw that the stricken whale was surrounded by four others, who stuck so closely beside him that Captain Wicks could not get up alongside his prize to give him the first thrust of the deadly lance without great danger. At last, however, this was attempted, but the whale was not badly hurt, and the four other fish at once sounded as they smelt the creature's blood.

"But suddenly, to Martin's horror, the huge head of an enormous bull shot up from the ocean, directly beneath the captain's boat! The fearful jaws opened and closed and crushed her like an eggshell. For-

tunately Wicks and his crew sprang overboard the moment they caught sight of that
tremendous head, and none were killed,
although two were injured. Martin at once
picked them up. Meanwhile the cause of
the disaster darted away after his three
companions and the wounded fish, which
was lying on the surface spouting blood
(much to Martin's satisfaction, for he feared
that the infuriated creature would destroy
his boat as well as that of Captain Wicks).
The condition of the injured men justified
Martin in making back to the ship, seeing
that another boat from the brig was hasten-
ing to kill the wounded whale. Hastily
putting Captain Wicks and his men on
board his ship, Martin again started out to
meet the 'loose' whales, which were now
coming swiftly down towards the ships.
The big bull which had destroyed Wicks'
boat was leading, the others following him
closely. Suddenly, however, he caught
sight of Martin's boat, swerved from his

course, and let his companions go on
without him. Then he hove to—as if
awaiting the boat and disdaining to escape.

"But just as Martin came within striking
distance and called out 'Stand úp!' to the
harpooner, the whale sounded, only to
reappear in a few minutes within a few
yards of the boat, rushing at it with open
jaws and evidently bent upon destroying it
and its occupants. So sudden was the
onslaught that Martin only saved himself
and his crew from destruction by slewing
the boat's head round as the monster's jaws
closed; but as leviathan swept by he gave
the boat the much-dreaded 'under clip'
with his flukes, and tossed her high in the
air, to fall back in the water a hopelessly
stove-in and shattered wreck. And then,
to the terror of the crew, as they clung to
the broken timbers, the whale returned, and
the men had to separate and swim away,
and watched him seize the boat in his jaws
and literally bite it to pieces, tossing the

fragments away from him far and wide.
Then after a minute's pause, he turned over
and began swimming on his back, opening
and shutting his jaws and trying to discover
his foes.   For five minutes or so he swam
thus in widening circles, and then, as if
satisfied he could not find those he sought,
he turned over on his belly again and made
off.   Almost immediately after, Martin and
his men were rescued by another boat.

"But the whale had not finished his work
of destruction, and as if goaded to fury by
the loss of his companions and the escape
of his human foes, he again appeared, about   .
twenty minutes later, close to the Hawaiian
brig.   Holding his head high up out of the
water, he swam at a furious speed straight
towards the ship.   The wind had now
almost died away, and the brig had scarcely
more than steerage way on her; but the
cooper, who was in charge, put the helm
hard down, and the whale struck her a
slanting blow, just for'ard of the fore-chains.

Everyone on board was thrown down by
the force of the concussion, and the ship
began to make water. Scarcely had the
pumps been tried when a cry was raised
'He's coming back!'

"Looking over the side, he was seen fifty
feet below the surface, swimming round
and round the ship with incredible speed,
and evidently not much injured by the
impact. In a few minutes he rose to the
surface about a cable's length away, and
then, for the second time, came at the ship,
swimming well up out of the water, and
apparently meaning to strike her fairly
amidships on the port side. This time,
however, he failed, for the third mate's boat,
which had had to cut from a whale to which
it had fastened, was between him and the
ship, and the officer in charge, as the whale
swept by, fired a bomb into him, which
killed him almost immediately. Only for
this he would certainly have crashed into
the brig and sunk her."

One of the most tragic and well-known affairs was the destruction by a sperm whale of the London whaler *Essex*, Captain Pollard, in 1820. An enormous bull twice charged her and crushed in her side. The crew took to the boats, and after dreadful sufferings some of the boats reached Valparaiso, but one which made Elizabeth Island (near Pitcairn Island) lost all her men but two.

The reader must bear in mind that these 'fighting' whales are the cachalot or sperm whales, a creature that is very different from the right or Greenland whale (from which baleen, or whalebone, is taken) or from any other of the cetacean family, such as the Humpback, the Grey, the Bottle-nosed, and the long and swift Fin-back. The capture of the latter is never attempted by whaleships, though they are the most plentiful of all whales. One reason for this is that the layer of blubber is thin, and although they have plates of baleen like the right whale, which is valuable, once they are

struck with a harpoon they dart off at such
a terrific speed that no boat could carry a
sufficient length of line to enable her to
hold on when the creature 'sounded'; the
line would have to be cut or the boat
carried below. I know of but one
place where these flying fin-backs
are captured, and that is at Twofold
Bay, in New South Wales. Here there is
a shore whaling station, and here, too, is
literally a 'resident' drove of those extra-
ordinary creatures the 'killers.' As the
schools of fin-back whales pass northward
to the Brampton shoals they hug the
Australian shore, and as they pass the heads
of Twofold Bay they are assailed by the
'killers,' which fasten to them like bull-dogs
and enable the shore boats to get up and
kill them with either lance or bomb. In
1894 one of these fin-backs became so
terrified at being pursued by 'killers' that he
dashed into the harbour, crashed into and
sank a yacht lying at anchor, then ran into

a jetty, which he badly damaged, and finally brought up on shore near the township of Eden. This whale was 57 feet in length— by no means a big 'finner,' for they exceed even the cachalot in length, though not in bulk. In 1890 the barque *John and Alton,* when cruising in the Great Australian Bight, killed a fin-back whale that was 90 feet in length. It approached the barque so closely that a bomb was fired into it from the deck. In 1896, while the writer was cruising after humpbacks in the steamer *Jenny Lind* of Sydney, we sighted a dead whale on shore in Wreck Bay. It had been driven ashore by 'killers,' and was too 'high' to be of any use. It measured over 72 feet in length.

PRINTED BY NEILL AND CO., LTD., EDINBURGH.

Lightning Source UK Ltd.
Milton Keynes UK
UKHW011441010219
336576UK00010B/708/P